Blacktime Song by Rosalie Wolfe

Marylee Daniel Mitcham

Eloquent Books
Durham, Connecticut

Eloquent Books
An imprint of Strategic Book Group
P.O. Box 333
Durham CT 06422
www.StrategicBookGroup.com

ISBN: 978-1-60911-497-8

Book Design: Bruce Salender

Printed in the United States of America.

To my husband, Carl, who helped me
with the crucial elements of storytelling
called starting and finishing.
Thank you dear, I love you. Marylee

Acknowledgments

Thanks to Peter Bonavich for letting me base a character on someone fictional, using his exact name; and thanks to Reedy Gibbs, who named her real daughter Meadow before I used it in a novel.
I hope you approve of the character, whom I created using four people not named Meadow!

Marylee Daniel Mitcham

Contents

Foreword

I have the privilege of writing the Foreword to two documents written years apart by the same woman, my mother, Rosalie Wolfe. One is a heretofore unpublished novella written in the 1970s and archived in a trunk. It is named *Hannah Wolfe's Blacktime Song,* and it is just barely fiction. The other is *Counting Down*: *A Memoir*, a contemporary work of nonfiction in which the author indicates she attempts to fill in and flesh out the novella. Both works have their own integrity, but together they are more whole than they would be alone.

If the reader begins with the novella, which I think is more satisfying, there will be a glitch. Who is Hannah Wolfe when she's first introduced on the page? What does she look like, and from what context did she drive to Kentucky? We don't find out much about that until we read Rosalie Wolfe's memoir and learn that, except for the fact Hannah's eyes are brown and Rosalie's are blue, they are the same short, intelligent, determined woman I recognize as basically one person. This is why I must say her story is barely fiction.

As readers we are asked to let go of many questions and invest in Hannah's point of view mid-stride, so to speak. We must surmise and give her a certain benefit of the doubt. She doesn't warn us that she's more intrigued with the unseen than the seen, with absence more than presence.

Eventually we realize Hannah connects to the unseen through listening, listening as though to a song, thus her title. Music for Rosalie Wolfe/Hannah is not just a motif — it's a way of perceiving reality.

•

I said that *Hannah Wolfe's Blacktime Song* is just barely fiction. For example, Rosalie chose not to disguise me at all as a fictional character. She named herself Hannah, but *me* she named Meadow. When it hits so close to home, I'm half-shocked at the power novelists have. Was she fair to me? I'm satisfied she was; perhaps she was more than fair. Certainly her love for me is quite evident.

My own memories of our year in Kentucky no longer seem contemporary at all, and are much less distinct than hers. Only two stand out, and the first is numinous still. On a night that was balmy and clear, we walked only by moonlight for what seemed like hours, but wasn't. She wouldn't tell me where we were going, but I remember being happy, and I also felt an exhilarated anxiety to be out so late on an errand that seemed mysterious.

Much of the time we walked along a paved road without any traffic at all. Finally, I saw the house that I realized we were walking toward. Our landlord lived there, and I won't divulge his real name. We did not knock at his door as I expected. Instead, we circled round to the side yard and looked in through an open window at the man himself. His cocker spaniel looked back at us, but didn't bark or get excited. He was an old dog and knew us well. That's all we did, look at J. Norris Simpson (as he's called in the book) for a few minutes, but those moments stayed with me because my mother was so reverent. Quite honestly, I had the feeling we were looking at Heavenly Father Himself because of the way she did it. And I was too young to understand it was a felony.

The other memory I still retain with some clarity is really an episode involving a disturbed young man (whose name is also disguised) and my use of a knife he gave me for play. The shame remains, but more as a memory than an active feeling. I was forgiven, starting with my mother. I must leave that story to the narrative. Someday I will unpack it, dust it off, and repack it according to my own memories. For parenting my two untamed sons, I will, no doubt, tell it with my head hung low.

•

As a Mark Twain scholar, I have thought long and hard about a cast of characters in the canon of 19th century literature. I see Hannah as a descendant of a type. Introspective though the character of Hannah is, she is no Virginia Wolfe. She functions more like Huck Finn in the world, staying just outside Aunt Polly's civilizing reach. Her comedy is raw, based on the freedom to have misadventures, to stay untutored (as opposed to willfully ignorant). Beneath her slapstick, as she apologetically calls it, lies a motivating desperation, but also within saving reach, the sheer gratuity of Existence Itself. For me her *Song* emerges as a kind of tone, something like a funky hum or a jazzy hymn. I like that sound for being deviant in the best sense.

•

This also might be the place to address Rosalie's account of my conversion at age fourteen to The Church of Jesus Christ of Latter-day Saints. She told it (almost) like it was, and I have to say I've never looked back. It was the best decision I've ever made in my life.

In some sense I am glad I was not born into the Church because that looks to me like a possible handicap. Some members grow up loyal and obedient in a personally non-integrated way. Then at some point in maturity, they realize they have doubts that have never been expressed, and can no longer go unvoiced. When this inner backlash comes, members sometimes judge themselves (and the Church) harshly, as though there is widespread fault. They feel both guilt and blame for having emotional or intellectual needs in the first place.

This is not primarily an institutional problem as I see it, but a personal one of needing to accept the inner movements of belief. It is human to seek and never stop seeking; to head out in new ways, mostly interior; to convert oneself more and more deeply as challenges are acknowledged and honestly faced, even for those born into this Faith.

Admittedly, my Church reveres the convert, whose bosom truly burns with truth. For the one who joins, all fish is fresh, none of it is frozen. These converts of record are often like the prodigal son whose shame melts away in the arms of the Father. Longstanding sons and daughters have it always available as well. But we forget sometimes that everything depends on our own personal desire and agency. We misguide ourselves if we ask the Church to give us that full equanimity offered only in direct relationship between ourselves and God.

Steadily, converts come in need and in hope to a place where, among other things even more important, they wrestle their differences into some kind of brotherly and sisterly conformity. But scratch any convert and you find a Hannah, someone who is at heart courageous, independent, and peculiarly sensitive to the Gospel of Jesus Christ. You will find a person born to love and serve God. It is the steady influx of these seekers after righteousness, and the convert spirit in so many other members, that continue to kindle my appreciation of the Mormon Church.

•

I hope you enjoy this work, Rosalie Wolfe's debut as a writer. It still surprises me since I knew nothing of her old manuscript until she completed the new one and shared them both with me. I felt a deeper kind of surprise than usual at my mother. It made me feel so giddy that I wanted to compose a song about giving up coffee. But if you want to understand that, you'll have to read her whole book.

Meadow Wolfe Dent
Brigham Young University
Provo, Utah
April 2004

Book I
Hannah Wolfe's Blacktime Song
Rosalie Wolfe

Worthy art Thou to be praised
Lord of honor and might
For Thou hast Earth and Heaven created
and for Thy good pleasure
all things have their being and are and were created.

—Rev. 4:11 and from Brahms: *A German Requiem,* Op. 45

1.

"If I die at night – "

Lying in bed, Hannah directed her remark to the ceiling. Or rather, she directed it to an unlimited expanse of black night now made invisible by the ceiling, tar papered black. "If I die at night," she repeated, like someone doing simple math, "it will be slapstick all the way. Slap. Stick."

In the heat, all her chigger bites itched and Hannah wondered if – given the drag of body and soul – she had enough will power to keep trying to fall asleep. It was just like her to start something she couldn't finish.

"Gotta be a saint to fall asleep," she mumbled, and heard, like an impudent reply, the strum of a guitar. It was *him* again, the Cowboy, that shiftless figment of her imagination. He said, "*I'll take a little hunky, Dorie.*" She hadn't even been asleep.

Last night he had serenaded her with a garbled rendition of the song "Blue Moon." She had no idea what he would sing tonight, but tried to dodge whatever it was with a desperate attempt at unconsciousness. It didn't work; apparently there's no rest for women who hear twangy voices.

> *I have sautéed my feelings,*
> *creamed my feelings,*
> *sautéed my feelings,*
> *just for you.*

"That's the most disgusting music I've ever heard," whispered Hannah to herself, still listening as the chords rolled out of nowhere into the pit of her stomach. Go *sauté your feelings* in some other frying pan!

2.

It was nearly Thanksgiving when she and Meadow moved to the Knobs Region of Kentucky last year. They had driven down from Cincinnati in the Old Blue Chevy, which had four new tires, part of Hannah's preparation for bad roads and country gravel.

"Our old ones would just pop," said Meadow. "It'd scare Antlers out of his pants. Bang! Bang! Bang!"

"Bang!" said Hannah. "Four tires, four bangs."

"You're 100 percent right," said Meadow, sounding like her mother. "Where's Antlers gonna sit? You didn't leave him a seat."

"Back there on top of our unprecious belongings."

"Poor kitty."

"Poor thing," agreed Hannah, in duet, as she stared at the car, "all the way to Kentucky sitting on a Foley Food Mill."

They both looked at the sagging car.

"See, the problem is, even when we try not to, we've got too much stuff. We'll probably get arrested for traveling this way. I'll look in my rear view mirror and all I'll be able to see is Antlers in a kitchen pan."

"Will the policemen put us in jail?"

"Nope."

Meadow nodded. She was a good listener. She was also suitably impressed that her mother understood these things.

"Are we gonna sleep in a real motel?" she asked.

"I'll have to see if the fake motels are cheaper," said Hannah, still gazing at the vehicle, passionately praying it would keep its torchlight burning. She considered how odd prayer was. The words themselves hardly mattered because God knew what you meant. He plumbed your murky depths with ease. And yet, words *seemed* quite necessary, even if absurd.

"You're not scared are you Meadow? I mean, does moving scare you?"

"Nope. I'm never scared to move. *Finally* we get to! I think it's gonna be fun to live in the woods. I'm gonna be real nice to all the wild animals so they'll be my friends."

Their long afternoon's ride was swift and contained, with scenery they never much noticed. To their right and left, land rolled by undisclosed, almost in eclipse, while they talked of something else, of Hannah's childhood mostly, which Meadow ranked high in terms of adventure.

"I haven't run away from home yet," Meadow told her mother, "but I'll have a story about selling our furniture and moving to Kentucky where the Indians and Daniel Boone lived on hills. And where our county looks like a horseshoe!"

"Sure enough," said Hannah. "Now finish that sandwich and help me look for real motels."

Obediently, Meadow took a bite of her sandwich and continued. "I'll tell my kids it was sort of like running away from home, only I did it with you because I didn't want you to go be poor all by yourself."

A selfless volunteer was more than Hannah's poise could manage, so she jerked the steering wheel as comically as possible, and pretended the car was out of control. At the end of her performance she said, "How come you think I'm going off to be poor?"

"Because you are," said Meadow. And then as if to state the even more obvious, "*God likes* poor people. You said so."

In the silences that ensued, Hannah concentrated on the road ahead, especially the one she was dragging Meadow down.

"I've gone and done it now," she decided, as they left Ohio behind. "I must be out of my mind. If only I'd had car trouble, I could have taken it as a sign to turn around.

3.

Grounded in ignorance, Hannah knew she would find a place to live as soon as she completed the obligatory motions. It seemed ritually correct that everyone had a home or found one. The end was sure. But it was necessary to do enough – to drive enough small back roads, to let enough dogs bark at you, to encounter enough people you would never see again. She trusted that out of this ceremony, a house, the one meant for her, would clearly emerge.

As it turned out, it was set back from the road against a heavily forested ridge and emerged as a disappointment, having none of the fairy tale charm she hoped for and Meadow expected. But it was hers. She knew by the way her heart sank at the inevitable, deliberate look of its boards. This was likely it.

No inquiry had led her there. She had spotted it the first day out, gray and weathered on a slope. It was, indeed, a tumbledown shack with a slight forward tilt indicating, perhaps, the direction it would one day fall. In a good high wind, she thought, it might hit the road where she was parked. She got out of her car and climbed a barbed wire fence to investigate. When nothing ripped, she congratulated herself on a useful skill and marched unevenly up the hill.

Unfortunately, the house itself was not in the woods as she had promised. On the contrary, it sat amid stumps from which the woods were violently missing. But it did have one large shade tree, which upon closer inspection proved to have shaggy bark and a few shriveled leaves. She'd settle for that. The tree was alive, the shack had *some* character, and it was set back from the road away from neighbors, which was precisely what she wanted. The whole thing seemed plausible. Besides, an entire forest cradled the amputated hillside, so she wouldn't have to forfeit her romance with the trees.

Trees, not alleys. They had moved to the sandstone knobs of Kentucky!

Back in the car, a dowdy, shivering Hannah peered at the house from the road again. Lucky for her, she'd left Meadow, her talisman in reserve, with a babysitter at that ridiculous, truly-fake-Western motel. A few hours of television at "The Yumaville" couldn't do much harm, and this way she could prepare the child for the rawness of their real situation. No thatch, no stone hearth, no geese – those were only in the storybooks. Besides, they hadn't made this crazy move to find a perfect cottage. Or she guessed they had, and this was it; an off-kilter house stupidly balanced at one end on old tires. You couldn't depend on such a house; you'd have to depend on something else that was hidden, and more unexpected. This was what Hannah wanted and had to do, never mind her sometimes sinking heart. Never mind that she hadn't rented the place yet. It would work out. She'd drive along the fence line until she came to someone; she'd ask until she found out whatever she needed to know.

The Chevy started again with easy confirmation, almost like the old days when her every movement, her every initiative, leafed and flowered. She couldn't help but notice. And it was also fortuitous that the neighboring house proved closer than half a mile. White and two-storied, it was nicer than most she'd seen. Down this way, the houses looked squatty and made her think, if not of criminals, then of people on parole.

Regretful to leave the stale warmth of her car, Hannah summoned a patient knock for the farmhouse door, one last obligatory motion performed in great need of a hot cup of coffee. She was not the least surprised to meet a man named J. Norris Simpson who said he owned the empty place up the hill and agreed to rent. He was slow to agree to anything, but when he did, he said he'd take fifty dollars a month, a price she could afford for at least a year. Poverty was expensive and she'd had to save up. Too bad, she thought, it wasn't cheaper to be poor.

4.

On a sweltering day in late August, Hannah woke reluctantly to the noises of a stuck drawer, three scrapes out and a loud slam shut; the vibrations set her gently rocking. Grating of drawers always came from Meadow's room, the only bedroom in the house. Hannah herself slept in the front room, where there were no bureaus, on a couch, which she usually unfolded. Pulled out it was reminiscent of a hammock, only bigger. With no place under which to tuck covers, it seemed improvised, no matter what.

Meadow's bed was better. Hannah had even built it herself, making the frame (absolutely no squeaks or sags) out of poplar floor boards and limestone block. The materials were scavenged at great cost to her back from the rubble of a once stately house just over the county line. But it was worth it. In the throes of any mood whatever, you could fling yourself down on Meadow's bed, and it didn't conjure up a cheap motel.

With its Moon-Over-The-Mountain quilt, it was a classy bed. Admittedly, her chest of drawers was not. It was swollen shut in the summer heat and the veneer was peeling off, but the bed was superior, like Meadow herself.

"Hi, Mama Wolf!"

A vivid but delicate child hopped from one room into the next with dramatic flair, offering her mother a look at ten fingers.

"I got ready for school. All by myself. I even cleaned my fingernails."

"Hi, Meadow Mouse Wolfe. Guess what, today's Saturday."

Since her hands were in the air anyway, she swung them over her mouth in a hammy gesture of 'oops.' Then she explained.

"Antlers woke me up."

"Antlers doesn't know too much about Saturdays, does he?"

Meadow thought about it. "Antlers is only two years old, and you don't get to be in first grade until you're six, so he doesn't know about a lot of things yet."

"Right," said her mother. "He's still a smart cat. Plus, he's the biggest, most beautiful yellow cat you and I have ever known and he'd probably win a contest if we put him in one."

"Right," seconded Meadow. They enjoyed their agreement.

"Hey, freckle-face, come hop in bed with me and I'll snuggle you. I love to snuggle people with clean clothes on who've cleaned their fingernails."

Hannah's daughter closed her eyes and felt her way over. She wore a yellow pinafore with blue jean cutoffs for underwear, to keep the boys' minds calm. It was a school rule that the girls had to wear shorts under their dresses.

Her dark curly hair, badly brushed, was tied with a black ribbon, and underneath it her neck was already damp from the heat of another humid morning. Winter weather was almost three months away, cold mornings half that. Hannah wasn't ready.

Meadow pushed her stem-like body back against her mother's, and they both lay staring in the same direction, toward a long, white sink and rusty cook stove. Antlers was crouched anxiously near the compost bucket, waiting for breakfast. Even in summer he liked to stay hidden under one of two wood stoves (the second, a potbelly for heating), but this time of day he made himself visible. His whiskers twitched irritably at the delay of his meal.

Hannah caressed Meadow's hair, as though readying it for school. Her head still smelled like lemon candy. It had since birth. No other baby she'd ever held smelled the same, not one of them as good. Maybe she *was* a mama wolf, knowing her own by instinct.

"I couldn't braid my hair. I *wish* you'd teach me. Please? I'm the only girl in my class who doesn't know how."

"We could practice on your doll. How does that sound?"

"Nope. I've decided I don't want her anymore. She's too dead."

"That's silly talk. She was never alive."

"Was she born dead?"

"She wasn't *born*, Goose. That's the goofiest question I ever heard. Why are you talking so goofy?"

"Hey Ma, you know what? I made up a song before I went to sleep last night. I sang it over and over to Antlers, and I still remember it. You wanna hear?"

Hannah liked to be called 'Ma'. It was an affectation that suited her, one that Meadow had readily picked up at the Simpson house. J. Norris called his wife 'Ma' along with the boys. Meadow called Mrs. Simpson 'Ma' too, and it had recently dawned on her that she had a 'Ma' of her own.

"Sure. I'm the perfect audience for any song you make up. Shoot. I mean, sing."

"It's about coffee."

"Doesn't sound too promising, but you never know. It can't be any worse than most of the songs that come to me."

Meadow wiggled out of Hannah's arms and took up a dreamy position in the middle of the room. She held a pretend microphone in front of her face and gazed with ardor into a pretend audience. Hannah groaned inwardly at such obvious evidence of television. Meadow watched it at Simpson's on special occasions.

"Oh my coffee is too hot
so I put some salt in it
to cool it down.
Now my coffee is too salty.
Oh, oh, oh.

"So I put some sugar in it
to take away the salt
and now
my coffee is too salty
and too sweet,
Oh, oh, oh."

"God, how I love that child," thought Hannah, and felt a sudden stab of deep and mixed emotion that resembled fear.

> "So I put some butter in it
> (margarine will do just fine)
> to thicken it up
>   and now...
> my coffee is too cold,
> it's too salty and too sweet,
> it's too thick and I wish
> I'd left it like it was.
> Oh, oh, oh."

Meadow lowered her microphone and bowed to waves of pretend applause.

"Very good, Meadow. I liked it a lot. A whole bunch."

"Now you sing one!"

"Nope, I'm not used to microphones and audiences."

"You can lie right here and sing in bed. Please, Ma! This is fun, it's your turn now." She looked at Hannah with fond conspiracy from which there was no escaping.

"Okay, one measly little song, and then it's no more bed until tomorrow night. Daylight's a'wasting!"

Meadow nodded, shivering with excitement.

"Ready? Hold still now, little girl or I won't be able to think."

> "J. Norris Simpson's a squinty old man,
> washed his face in a frying pan,
> combed his hair with a wagon wheel,
> cried with a toothache in his heel.
>
> Get out of the way, old J. Norris,
> take your rent and leave my forest,
> keep your money, but leave me be,
> I'm sick to death of your old T.V."

"Good, good, that's good! You can really make up good songs!"

"Well, I didn't make it up, I just borrowed it."

"I never knew J. Norris had a song about him!"

"That's the part I made up. It's really about Old Dan Tucker."

"Who's he?"

Hannah sighed. "Come on now, it's time to get up. Heave ho." She pushed Meadow off the bed. "Take a look at Antlers over there. He's so hungry, he can hardly stand it. Feed him one of those cold pancakes from yesterday."

"He doesn't like pancakes. I'll catch him some fish."

"Okay, use a pancake for bait. *Little* pieces. If you throw it in all at once, it'll just sink."

Looking back she remembered J. Norris as not so bad. True, his eyes watered some as he stood at the door talking to her, but she assumed it was the sudden rush of cold air on his face. She wouldn't have called it a squint or presumed he had any character faults, past not inviting her in.

He seemed fine. Fifty-ish and overweight with thin yellow-gray hair combed to hide his baldness. She never expected to get to know him at all, so it was in that sense he seemed fine. Since he was not a large part of her life and never would be, she allowed him his initial curiosity which, of course, she refused to satisfy. Her only concession was nonchalance – allowing him the privilege of sniffing about, surmising this and conjecturing that. After all, strangers had to expect a modicum of curiosity, and any outsider who waltzed onto an insider's porch (expecting a key!) was a likely figure for the imagination.

She introduced herself as Hannah Wolfe, a woman with one child. When they had finished their business, he was calling her Misrus Wolfe. Such conventional imagination seemed quite in order. But that was nine months ago. Something else was happening now and conventional or not, it disquieted her beyond measure. Her feelings toward Simpson wouldn't sort themselves out. Sometimes she felt pure rage, which wasn't called for. He'd never so much as laid a hand on her or even spoken out of line, but she felt hunted, like she was down a hole somewhere and he was sniffing and whining above. His teary eyes assaulted her. Even his fingernails seemed too much to bear. They were long and square at the top, very hard. When they hit against things, they made noise.

She wished he would make his real intentions known so she could decide conclusively what she thought about him. As it was, she couldn't quite figure him out.

Even on that first day, she couldn't read the looks he gave her, not that she thought about it then; she was too excited about the house. But what did he have to bob around about? Fifty dollars a month? It wasn't like he'd been eager to rent.

One thing was certain, he had wanted her to understand that he was fed up with former trashy tenants and would rather "burn the house down hisself" than see "liquored-up scum" abuse his property. He didn't rant, but he spoke like a man who knew his lines, who had rehearsed until he'd gotten them right.

He must have decided she wasn't scum, or she wouldn't have gotten the place. But there was a warning in his voice too, one she'd made every effort to allay by adopting a high-tone, teetotaler air that contrasted oddly with her shivering appearance in less than warm clothes.

She had never found reason to doubt his integrity. He wasn't dirty or profane. He was reliable and she never caught liquor on his breath. As far as she could tell, he and his family lived a model country life. Even the teenage Simpson boys were sober and hardworking, both the kind of boys to bring their mother yard ornaments. No, if J. Norris Simpson had a secret lowlife (she'd bet her eyeteeth he did), he was crafty about it. He didn't let it infringe on his early rising and mowed lawn.

Moving stiffly and sighing loudly like a woman on stage, Hannah got out of bed. Bed was her major consolation unless she stayed in it too long, which made her ache all over. Sometimes she wondered how it could be that bed, being such a consolation, was her most desperate place. It was in bed she always made her worst cute remarks and thought about dying. Bed might be the best place to die, but she wasn't ready.

To emphasize the truth of that sentiment, Hannah decided to take off her nightgown, a positive step in the wholesome direction of getting dressed. It was a pink summer nightie, very prim, the kind of ensemble her mother, Lucille, often gave as a gift. The matching slippers had long since worn out because she was in the habit of dashing outside in them or telling Meadow to slip them on to keep her feet dry on her way to the outhouse.

City clothes in the country were foolish, but they were better than going naked. That would only make her feel lonely. Sometime, if she ever got her hands on more money, she'd buy one or two good things she needed, whatever those people bought who walked the Appalachian Trail. Camping gear, the kind that lasts. A down jacket for winter.

Hannah squeezed her arm above the elbow and patted herself across the breasts imagining a puffy green jacket stuffed with the finest of feathers. She wanted to look in a mirror, but she'd given the only decent one she owned to Good Will the week she'd left town. The shard she brought to Kentucky was large enough for winter use, but only showed her wild auburn hair and sandy complexion, which reminded her of those "Portuguese-Indian" photos Lucille kept hidden. Yep, a sorry brown-eyed countenance clenched with cold and no longer lovely.

"Wale, Misrus Wolfe," she said aloud to herself. She put her hands on her hips and wished again for a mirror, the better to see old granny. "Here you stand, hot and neck-ed as the slope you live on, and all you kin worry about is Old Man Winter and your lost looks, which you ain't got a man to care about no how."

She had been without men a long time, ever since she got pregnant with Meadow. Renouncing promiscuity was an abyss she stared into, contemplating the depth of, who knows? Forty more years … way way down there? Right now a man wouldn't be too bad, the kind you'd walk the Appalachian Trail with. But who was on the scene besides Simpson, except that idle cowpoke who pestered her at odd hours? It was a toss-up what thought depressed her more, Old Man Winter or Old Man Simpson. Or Old Man God, for that matter. He was supposed to have been waiting in Kentucky. Winter sure as hell was!

You betch your invisible britches!

Who asked you? You shut your invisible mouth!

Winter, Simpson, and God. They were her three miserable subjects to brood on. She couldn't help herself, she was plagued. If it weren't for Meadow, she'd probably go mad. Stark-naked, raving mad.

Grimacing like a lunatic, she grabbed her clothes, which were tidily portioned out on a row of nails she had hammered into the wall. Grimy or not, she was wearing them. That well-worn mumble of hers was still a serviceable excuse: Washing clothes by hand is no joke.

Dirty blue jeans didn't faze her, but she whipped a light blue T-shirt over and off her head in one motion of revulsion. Smelly T-shirts were no joke either. She'd have to get a clean one out of the trunk or she'd never be able to stand herself. Suddenly her mood was black as dirty fingernails because of Winter and Simpson and God.

Winter: She hadn't adjusted to her environment nearly as well as the Chevy. After a couple of rough months, it followed the local custom of dying and spent the winter near the gully down from the house. It had weathered each frozen day amicably enough, just like the beer cans strewn along the road, and in the spring it had been a prominent, almost cheerful, spot of blue. She hardly noticed it now – perhaps she had adapted some.

But the cold, who could adapt to it, to waxy-white feet, to fingers so numb they might as well be missing? One time her hands felt expanded and queer. When she looked down at them, she was invited to ponder a row of mottled fingers, some purple and some a dull yellow. It was hard to tell which color would fall off first.

Meadow fared better because she relaxed and trusted her mother to keep them warm. It was simple. If the fire in either stove burned low, and the woodpile was gone, Hannah split more logs. Then if Meadow were cold, she got into bed. If she were still cold, she got Antlers and a hot water bottle in bed with her, one on each side. Cold nights, Hannah's warm tears were not upsetting. But those tears, you had to watch out for them; they fell into the coffee.

Simpson: She couldn't have made it through the winter without his help. When the Chevy gave out, he packed her around in his four-wheel drive truck, an arrogant vehicle that broke its path to her door in all kinds of weather, for whatever reason. In winter it roared to her rescue at no charge with loads of firewood cut along the widening slope's edge. Simpson and son outdid each other in emptying the load from behind. They would have split it too, but she refused, unwilling to owe -- what *felt* like -- the company store and its loud, square-nosed machine.

God: Why didn't half a ton of number nine coal fall like manna from heaven? Why didn't those stingy trees volunteer to fall over and break up in pieces by themselves? She deeply regretted the massive, uncooperative spirit of nature, at least in moments of winter misery, certainly not her better moments.

Six years ago, her relationship with God was not so absurd. She was sure He *had* broken through to her in some inexplicable way, giving her a certainty that rang, true as chimes. He was there, strange and personal, beckoning her, suggesting Himself.

The impression in its pure form was fleeting, but about that time her daughter was born. She arrived like an emissary. Her very flesh glowed with primal light, and if her small infant's cry was not like the sound of chimes, it was nevertheless truer than anything else her mother had ever heard. It called her beyond herself to acknowledge the Maker of Infants.

Had a miniature sun been given her as alms, had it dropped before her eyes like a gold coin into her hand, Hannah Wolfe could not have felt more awed and destined to know Him. Six years ago, a very long time.

5.

"There's a redneck at the pond and he's eating Antler's pancake!"

Hannah reflected that life was, indeed, unpredictable – even cramped, boring lives like hers. She challenged Meadow with one eyebrow, asking herself what rednecks, pancakes, and cats could possibly have in common. The trio hardly seemed real; it was too patterned, like one of Meadow's songs.

"Is he eating it down on the ground like a wild man?" Hannah asked.

"No, he's pinching it – in little bitty pieces. And when I tell him to quit, he won't."

"Well, what do you say I go dunk his head?"

"Hurry, hurry before he's gone!"

The pond was Meadow's favorite place to play, though she sometimes had to share it with Simpson's strayed livestock. It had always been an ugly wet hole to Hannah, brown and murky like watercolors smeared together by an artless child. It seemed to have no setting of its own, was merely gouged from the hillside about the same distance from the road as her house.

Gradually the wind had brought it life, blowing cattails and a few puny willows into its shallows. Hannah wondered how these things happened. Did frogs migrate from distant marshes? She saw a line of them, eastern-born beyond the road, heading west, into the setting sun and toward her pond. And what about the minnows? Did tiny eggs come sailing through the air like seeds? However it was, nature had claimed it and so had Meadow, originally in disappointment over the elusive wild animals she wished to befriend.

Holding Meadow's clammy hand, Hannah strode two hundred yards and silently confronted a young and exceedingly thin man stretched out on the ground and propped on his elbow. She stood facing him while he continued to stare moodily at the water, as though he were alone and deeply lost in thought.

She could tell at first glance he wasn't a redneck, but in her own way, Meadow was right. His glistening neck was red as rouge – and no wonder – dressed as he was in a long-sleeved, plaid shirt in blazing sunshine. Even the plaid was red, a crimson grill that wavered in the heat.

Meadow's mistake would have been more amusing had he deigned to look up. In the face of such blatant posturing, she paused, but Meadow was quick to speak, as though reading a story. "And he ate it *all* up!"

With showy effort he disengaged himself from the water to deal with the child's accusation.

"I did not. I threw it to the fish."

"Who are you?" asked Hannah.

"Something that fell from the sky?" he suggested. This time even Meadow paused.

"Don't stare at me like that. Can't you take a joke?"

"I asked you who you were, not where you came from." She tried to decide what was wrong with his cheekbones.

"It so happens I'm a neighbor. From over the ridge. I think you know as much about me now as I do about you. Is that your … place of residence over there?"

"Look, you scared my daughter. This is private property and you'll have to explain yourself if you want any sort of welcome." It was his hair, or lack of it. It was cropped so close, his cheekbones took over his face.

"He didn't scare me, he just ate my pancake. I think he's pretty weird." Meadow furrowed her brow, contriving an adult expression of concern. She seemed to make an impact.

"I admit it, I admit it," he said, sitting up and placing one hand over his heart. "I admit to being pretty weird, and on top of that, I'm in an irritable mood today so the natural man is exaggerated. You'll have to excuse me. I'm harmless, I assure you. I don't normally alarm little girls. I was only …" He lowered his head to search for a word.

"Playing around?" said Meadow.

"That's right," he said. "I was trying to make friends with you. I think you're …"

"Lonesome?" supplied Meadow.

"No, I was going to say 'ingenious'." He smiled apologetically and looked at Hannah. "There's something intriguing about your daughter. Surely I'm not the first person to mention it?"

Hannah nodded, half forgiving. She didn't think he was dangerous.

"Where did you say you lived?" she asked him.

"Just over the ridge, a two-hour hike. I live with some potters." He raised his hand in a hasty oath. "Harmless potters, I assure you. A religious group of people."

"What are potters?" asked Meadow.

"One of them owns the piece of property," he continued. "To tell you the truth, I'm very thirsty. Could you spare me a drink of water? It was actually just luck I came upon your daughter."

Hannah only looked at him, debating what to do. Of course he must need a drink of water. But she couldn't decide.

"For pity sake, I'm only asking for a drink! Don't tell me you're afraid of the men around here? This isn't Manhattan, you know!"

His petulance displeased her, but after all, water was not a lot to ask for. She hated feeling indecisive.

"What'd you say your name was?" The question sounded so lame, she knew it would be her last.

"Ian."

"Okay, Ian," she concluded, taking Meadow's hand and starting home. "We've decided to invite you to our place of residence over there."

After a few steps she raised one hand and turned back in his direction. "I want you to know this part of the forest is religious too, and you're about to get some religious water."

He seemed thrown into confusion.

"She's just playing around," said Meadow. "Come on."

Hannah was grateful for the silence on their return because living in the county had worn her patience thin, contrary to what she had expected. She wasn't in the mood for conversation. It didn't seem propitious when he followed her through the door and headed comfortably for a stool, nor did the critical appraisal he gave it help. His silence lasted longer than her gratitude. Who was he to criticize her furniture? He was spindle-legged and flimsy himself.

She refused to ask him if he were a craftsman, but turned her back on him instead and reached into the shelf for cups. One at a time she dipped them in a bucket of clean drinking water. Simpson brought her five gallons twice a week.

"Here." Hannah thrust water at him in the name of the Maker of Infants. He made a little bow, then accepted and downed the liquid in one trembling movement. "Sorry it's not cool," she added. "No, wait, I haven't used up my ice cubes today." Out of a decrepit gas refrigerator, she took a metal tray of six cubes. "Two for you, two for Meadow, and two for me." She plunked them in his empty cup. "Want some more?"

"I'll do without ice if you'll be so kind as to fill this up repeatedly."

"Why don't I just get you an empty mayonnaise jar?"

"Not the one we pee in," mouthed Meadow so he couldn't hear.

"There's another kid over where I live named 'Willow'. You mothers seem to have a thing about nature. Not that I *don't*." He thought for a minute then continued in a huskier tone. "I'm not finished here yet."

"Oh brother," she mouthed, facing away, "another conundrum."

"Do you live here alone? Where's your, uh, husband?"

"Just me and my daughter."

"Meadow and?"

"Hannah Wolfe. What's your name?"

"I already told you."

"Ian what?"

"I don't tell people my last name."

Meadow giggled, and Ian turned sulkily in her direction. "It seems to me that anyone with a name such as 'Meadow Wolfe' – he pronounced the syllables with feigned difficulty – is better off not laughing over the name of someone else."

"I wasn't laughing at your name, I was laughing at your no name!"

Hannah giggled, and Ian gave her the same dirty look.

"Drink up, Ian. The day's half over and I have work to do."

"Could I be of any help?"

"Not a bit."

"I already confessed once to being weird."

"I don't care if you divulge your name or not, but I don't think you have any reason to be so touchy. We didn't exactly dash out there and capture you."

"Despite what you might think, I can take a hint. But thanks again for the cold drink of water." He faintly bowed a second time, then ran a hand over his shorn skull. He cleared his throat and looked at Meadow who was sitting cross-legged on the floor highly engrossed. "I'll hike over this way again and bring your cat another pancake. He's a superb cat. Very spiritual."

Meadow giggled nervously, but he seemed not to notice. As soon as he was out the door she asked about the harmless potters.

"Can we walk over the ridge and see them?"

"I don't think so. You know, he probably needed salt as well. I should have offered him a sandwich. He has a long walk back."

"I wonder what they look like?"

"Hey little girl, how about a kiss?" Hannah reached for Meadow, her perfect child.

6.

It was September before he showed up again, though only a week to the day since she'd seen him last. The change in humidity gave him a history, coming as he had at the height of sultry weather, and now again when the air was drier and inhaling seemed to do more good.

A break in the heat wave didn't mean it was pleasant to hear him knocking on the door. Meadow had stepped from the washtub, and Hannah was wrapping her dripping daughter in a towel when he interrupted. Until that moment, the morning had been charmed.

"Come on in before you break the door down," she yelled, raising her voice as though he were banging. She'd heard no truck coming up the slope, so knew who it was even before the door swung open revealing Ian, pancake in hand.

"It's the delivery boy, come to make a better impression than last time. Does your cat like buckwheat griddle cakes?" He smiled first at Hannah, then at Meadow, handing her his peace offering, which she accepted with a crooked grin.

"Hi, Ian! Ma told me we couldn't walk over there even if I want to. Which I do want to."

"I said *probably* not." It sounded to Hannah like Meadow now considered him a friend of the family. She'd done the same with Simpson, immediately accepted him at face value. "After all, we don't even *know* Ian and his friends, Meadow. It takes a long time to get to know people."

"You tell your mother," whispered Ian, leaning over the door sill, "that it's not healthy to stay at home and mope, and that you don't get to know others unless you make a slight effort."

She'd left herself wide open for that one. "I don't mope," sang Hannah, "and I also don't visit."

"I get to know people pretty quick," said Meadow.

"Quicker than she should," countered Hannah. "Come on in and shut the door, Ian."

"You're sure I'm welcome?"

"Well, let's put it this way. Fate seems to have introduced us. So have a seat on what I hope is my plenty-good-enough floor." She waved her hand to indicate it, a domain to which he was welcome, at least for now. If nothing else, she welcomed the new and better sunlight in which he stood framed and gleaming.

"Meadow, go put your clothes on, Babe."

"Ian, watch me. I'm a Meadow Hopper!" Still wrapped in her towel, she hopped out of the room. From the bedroom she called back, "Show him the fish, Ma!"

"What fish?" he asked, looking around as if it had followed him in.

Hannah pointed to the tub of water, and he looked down. "Does your daughter always bathe with a fish?"

"Only on the days she can do without soap."

"I see," he replied, biting his cuticle. "Perhaps I *had* better close the door before the neighbors see what goes on here." He finally closed the door and Hannah couldn't tell if he were trying to imitate the reaction of a nervous man or not. Then he sat down on the floor. He was so thin, he seemed to collapse cleverly like a piece of portable equipment.

Uncomfortable, Hannah stood back up. "No, that's alright, stay put," she said. "I'll get you a jar of water. Are you as thirsty as last time? Could you use a sandwich?"

He reached for the pancake Meadow had left on the floor and looked it over. "This is only fit for a fish. It tasted good at breakfast."

"Peanut butter or cheese?"

"Peanut butter, please. And no, I'm not as hot as last time. It's not as humid."

While Hannah was making his sandwich, she let the thread of conversation drop. She thought about the weather a lot, but felt it was inane to discuss it the way everyone always did.

"Did I ever mention that Ian's just a nickname?"

"No, what's your full name?"

"Sebastian. 'Ian' is the last three letters, Sebast-*Ian*."

"Very dignified. Sebastian what?" she said, twisting the bread bag shut and turning to receive his answer.

He looked taken aback, as though she had hit him with a paper wad. His expression jolted her memory.

"Oh, I'm sorry, you already told me. You don't give out your last name."

"I've been in Kentucky since March and I haven't even given out 'Sebastian' until this morning."

"I don't understand why you'd keep it a secret."

"I suppose you haven't any secrets?" He had her there. "Besides, it isn't a secret, it's a preference."

"Oh. Well, that explains it," she said, handing him the sandwich. "I almost cut this four ways. That's how Meadow likes them."

"Thanks, Ma," he said, taking the halves. "How old are you, anyway? I'm nineteen. See? Now you know my age."

"I'm an old lady. I'll be twenty-six next year."

"I prefer old ladies, actually."

"Don't prefer them too much," she said very brightly. "How about another sandwich?"

He cleared his throat, shook his head no, and ran his hand over his head in a gesture she remembered. In fact, she wouldn't be surprised if he'd taken a secret vow of chastity. He looked like the kind who would, totally in his head.

Sebastian ate in silence, an awkward, but observant guest. In spite of herself, Hannah found him an interesting presence in the room – some brand of seeker, she told herself, mesmerized by his hands, which evidently trembled almost all the time. She tried to be surreptitious. Now that the door was closed he'd lost his gleam and ... oh save her ... it was happening again ... he wasn't connected anymore. When she tried to look at him, it didn't work, she blew a fuse.

Back in Cincinnati, when she looked at people, she saw them. A Black woman in a blue dress was a Black woman in a blue dress, and she knew what both those entities were, human beings and garments. As objects they registered quite nicely along her nerve endings, caused no vertigo, no anxiety: God made women, women made dresses, the dress fit the woman, and the woman fit the street she stood on.

She tried once more to look at Sebastian, the sum total of his parts, but his long-sleeved shirt wouldn't settle down like a garment should. It wouldn't fit his body. His body wouldn't fit the street. Nothing registered nicely, not since she'd moved here to lead this simple life.

Secondhand shoes and secondhand clothes,
They all call me secondhand Rose,
They all think they're pretty smart,
But I don't have a secondhand heart.

Absently, Hannah took up the Cowboy's song and sang sotto voce about Rose. "Don't panic," she said, giving herself mental orders, "you can just wait it out. Whatever you do, don't panic or it'll get worse."

"You like country music?" Sebastian seemed to be studying her. That was a switch.

"Yeah. A lot of it stinks, though."

"What part of the country are you from?"

"I've been living in Cincinnati quite awhile."

"What possessed you to move to Kentucky?" It was bound to come, but why now?

"Huh?"

"What are you? Some hermit waiting for a revelation?"

"What's that got to do with country music?"

"Anyone with a garden like yours hasn't gone back to the land. My impression is that you're on some sort of spiritual trip."

Secondhand shoes and secondhand mush,
They all call me secondhand flush,

"Listen, Sebastian, I don't mean to be rude, really I don't, but I can't sit around and gab all morning. Meadow! What's taking you so long? Are you dressed?"

"Here I come. I wanna show Ian something."

Straightaway, she popped into the room with a Job's Tears necklace wrapped around her head for a crown, and her mother's long, flounced cotton skirt pulled up to her armpits.

"Oh my gosh, what are you up to? We've gotta get to work."

"It's me, a singer! My name is Meadow Lark. You wanna hear me sing?" She reached for her pretend microphone. "Hey, fishy," she said, looking in the tub of water, "you wanna hear a fancy lady sing?"

Sebastian blushed, but rose to the occasion. "How many Meadows are there?" he asked with Herculean spontaneity. If he stretched his smile much farther, it would snap and hurt someone.

"Just only one," she declared. "But when I wanna be plain, I call myself Meadow Mouse and when I wanna be fancy, I call myself Meadow Lark and when I wanna be silly, I call myself Meadow Mush."

"Don't forget old Meadow Hopper," he admonished, eyeing the door.

"Yeah, when I wanna hop!"

Secondhand shoes and secondhand mush,
They all call me secondhand flush,
They all think they're pretty smart,
But I don't have a secondhand fart.

Hannah felt sticky and knew her T-shirt was on its way to being soaked with sweat, a distress signal she didn't want to send. Everything seemed so complicated. Didn't she have enough plagues without adding a parasite that drooled tunes? She felt invaded. "I *am* invaded," she inwardly wept, wiping wet palms on her jeans and leaning forward so her absorbent shirt wouldn't give her away as severely distressed. Now the beads of perspiration trickled down the hollow between her breasts and melted uncomfortably in the cloth at her waist.

At least he wouldn't notice. If she were going to lose her mind, she didn't intend to do it in front of anyone – not Sebastian, not Meadow.

"Listen guys," she drawled, feeling like her voice was being piped in from somewhere else. "I have *got* to get to work."

Meadow lowered her microphone with disappointment as Sebastian quickly stood up.

"Meadow, don't forget the fish. It's time he went back in the pond."

"Why?"

"You know why."

"Because he's about to die?"

"If you put him back in the pond, he won't."

Meadow got a jar and scooped him out of the tub. Then she pushed past Sebastian who had opened the door to leave.

"I could split some wood for you. They tell me that winter is on the way. How about plastic on your windows?"

"Since when is the first week of September almost winter?" She tried to sound lighthearted. Winter was something that happened to you when you were old, but she was young and carefree.

"At the very least," he continued, "autumn is on the way. The sky's that lovely shade of blue, that's how you know."

"What are you anyway? Some kind of long-sleeved nut who can't tell when summer's here? Some kind of Brazil nut or walnut who's on a 'lovely shade of blue' trip?"

He recoiled in amazement and her conscience went off like a fire alarm. It made a louder clang than any of the other noises in her head.

"Look, I'm terribly sorry … it's just that I don't feel like talking right now. I've been trying to let you know that I don't feel like talking at all right now because I have things to do, and this just isn't a good time for me. Now I know you mean well, which is more than I can say for myself – calling you a Brazil nut when all you offered was help – but for a moment I felt hopelessly upset and I said the first thing that came into my mind, which is exactly what I'm doing now, so I hope you'll forgive me."

When she finished, he didn't say anything so she began again. "Anyway, I'm really sorry and I appreciate your offer to split wood. Oh, and something else – there's really no need for either of us to explain how we wound up here or, you know, the big picture. I've got my secrets and you can have yours."

"I wear long sleeves because I have eczema. And I came to Kentucky because I was called by God."

"Oh." So much for his secret. He could say things like that if he wanted to.

"You know, Hannah, you're good for me, you are. I'm already convinced of it. We're very similar, even the irritable part. I've been looking for someone like you. I'll be back as soon as I can."

"Oh," she said again, nothing else coming to mind. The Cowboy had stopped singing and was apparently just listening in.

With that Sebastian turned a well-satisfied face to the door and left her. Some distance from the house he hooted at Meadow, trying to attract the child's attention. When he couldn't, he threw a rock into the pond, an efficient action. Watching from the doorway, Hannah saw her turn his way in time to catch an odd sort of victory salute he was giving.

The stiff way he waved his arm reminded her of winter. His gesture seemed inevitable. Perhaps that meant he was part of her life now, a friend of the family.

7.

Hannah heard him coming a long way off, as soon as he left the road and headed toward her. She had already heard the school bus squeal to a stop for Meadow down near his barn. It was a hulking shelter that expediently blocked the weather, though a legion of swarming flies decreased the value of its shade this last week of September. Later on, though, it would shield against the elements, breaking the wind before it sliced into her daughter's sound little body.

"It's only wind, for God's sake," said Hannah aloud, speaking vaguely upward, "the kind that blows through lilac bushes, helps birds fly, pushes paper boats, turns windmills in Texas!" But whatever innocuous words she toyed with as amulets, her own body remembered last year's chaotic onslaught, remembered it more as instinct than event. "A wind like that could carve initials on any child it chose," she whispered, and no voice from beyond corrected her.

In the wake of her afflicted thoughts, the pickup approached as though on cue with its depressing cargo, Simpson. The way he always drove too fast uphill infuriated her. Whenever he stopped by to visit, he slammed on the brakes about the time she decided he was literally passing through. And why he would park so close to the house, inches from the door, yet refuse to knock, was another equivocal dimension of his character. He had the not endearing trait of honking to announce himself. It was an accepted routine by now. She never walked out and shouted, "Am I deaf? Am I blind?" She gave, instead, the same crabby greeting.

"Why if it isn't J. Norris."

"Good morning, Hannah," he replied steadily, looking down at her from the cab of his truck. Besides the way he always reeked of hair oil, and said her name with too much self-indulgence, she disliked the way he kept it in his mouth. She wanted it off his tongue faster than he got it off. He wasn't so old and feeble he had to take it easy on her name.

"Did my check bounce?"

At this point he regularly climbed from his truck and said: "If it did, I don't know nothing of it."

Hannah watched him get out of the cab, but he didn't make his usual reply. Instead he hitched up his pants while the steady look lost its mooring. He was either preoccupied, or ill at ease, she couldn't tell which. His only reply was an embarrassed cough. Ill at ease, definitely. Hannah wondered if he *had* driven up to kick her out. When he tugged at his pants a second time, she knew things were serious. He wasn't being himself at all. To look at him now, you'd never know how nosy, probing and leering he was.

"Well, J. Norris, what's up? I've never seen you at a loss for words." He shifted from one leg to the other and looked at her miserably with that bloodshot squint of his before the thought hit her: Something debased is about to be revealed. He is going to make his underhanded proposal at last!

"Hannah," he began, "last evening I drew up the idea you could do me a favor."

"You did?" she said, wondering how to make a quick exit.

"I'm a peaceable man – you know it's the truth as well as anyone, now ain't it?" He straightened his shoulders as though waiting for a decoration. What a weasel!

"I guess so, J. Norris. As far as I *know* anyway."

"You're damned right I am – but pardon my language, Hannah. Another thing you know about me is that I don't hold with indecent talk in the presence of women folk."

"That's perfectly all right. I'm used to hearing men swear. Why, sometimes I even -- "

"Damn it," he said. "Right there's the trouble. I have a notion you are used to men. *Too* used to them. I sorely wish you hadn't saw fit to have men tramping up here."

Floored by the direction his remarks had taken, Hannah exercised her mouth for a moment before anything came out.

"Well, I, well … *goddamn it yourself*, J. Norris Simpson! *Just goddamn it yourself.*" She felt like spitting to show her disgust, but had never learned the art. "Who in the hell do you think you are?"

He made the barest attempt to answer, then shook his head like a public sinner.

"I no more have 'men tramping up here' than I have … really, Mr. Simpson, you are very far off base, and I find your insinuations to be ..." she paused for a breath, waiting on words extreme enough to show him the vileness of his suspicions. "They make me sick to my stomach."

At that she spun around, furious, on top of everything else, at her lack of deadliness. Escaping inside, she slammed the door, mortified to see it bounce back open. Before she could bring herself to try again, Simpson had closed it discreetly, all but where his hand was, and with his other hand he knocked like a perfect gentleman, too polite to look inside. Except for his fingers, the only thing she could see was his belly blocking the crack of light.

"Listen here, girl," he pleaded, breathing heavily through his nose. "You didn't give me any say. Come on out here and let me explain myself."

"Oh you explained yourself plenty," she said. "Go away."

"No sirree I didn't, Hannah. You got riled up too quick. I didn't even tell you that I had a horse to die. Somebody's killing my horses. Hear what I say? I'm duty bound to put a stop to it, any man would say the same. Git yourself out here, Hannah, this is pure business now. Horses ain't cheap and I can't afford to lose but one. I have to give you a couple notices to post, so git up off that sofa I gave you. Now listen, girl, I didn't mean nothing. You got riled up too quick." The man seemed to have found his tongue.

Yanking the door from his hand, she stared at him with a fierce, swollen, uncooperative expression. "Take your sofa when you leave."

He retreated to the pickup for the signs, fumbling under the seat for them. When he held them out to her, she gave him the meanest glare she could.

"You'll be doing me a big favor, Hannah, to nail these somewheres close to the house. You may not believe me, but there are hippies, nothing but hoodlums, that would just as soon shoot a horse as set on one. They'll be after my cows next, if they think they can get away with it."

Hannah nodded. "These sure are the very thing I need, No Trespassing signs. And how fortunate, here's a Posted: Keep Out. That certainly does express my wishes on the matter." She took the signs in one hand, holding them away from her body as though she were holding his dirty handkerchief.

"You can't trust every stranger that comes your way. Half of them is high on dope, Hannah. It's not safe for you or for Meadow, and I call it my duty to tell you so. I'm not just thinking of my own self." He still seemed edgy, though somewhat more confident, now that he'd gotten her to accept both signs.

"Mr. Simpson, it's ridiculous to expect me to post these on the house. These aren't meant for an occupied house, they're *fence* signs. Now you just take them down to the road where they belong."

"No, I didn't say they was for the house. Put one right on that tree there. Then find another tree up the ridge somewheres. You'll know the right spot."

"You find another tree. How the hell do I know which tree?" He looked pained at the currency of her language, accepting the one sign she now forced on him as her idea of a compromise.

"These knobs is full of youngsters, looks like they're from outer space. First one dropped down some five years ago, and now there's neighbors you've never seen the likes of. Never heard of their kin, not even the name of their kinfolks. I don't mind telling you, Hannah, they're trash mostly. Now that's my opinion and it ain't based on thin air because I've had them in this very house. I regretted it, I certainly did."

"Listen, Mr. Simpson, this place happens to be a dump. Living here leaves a lot to be desired, so don't go blaming me for your former tenants!"

"I was born in this house and we may have been poor, we most certainly were, but we weren't trash and that's a fact. If you ask me, a house resembles the folks who lives there and don't go getting riled up again because I've always thought you kept the place real tidy, and I'm not the one that called it a dump."

He looked like he might cry, a thoroughly unnerving look, so she swerved. "Listen, I bet hunters killed your horse. You know these knobs are crawling with hunters in and out of season. They're the ones that carry guns for God's sake! Someone just thought your horse was a deer and shot it by accident."

"It weren't no accident," he replied, thrusting his hand down into the pocket of his work pants where he had change to rattle. "That horse belonged to me, and a hundred to one they knowed it. You post that notice now. If any suspicious characters gives you trouble, I'll -- "

"I'll deal with them myself. I keep a baseball bat hidden away for just that purpose and believe me, I aim for heads."

When J. Norris Simpson climbed back in the truck, Hannah was sure he looked shaken.

Meadow wasn't used to finding Hannah in bed when she came home from school, but neither was she used to worrying. "Where's my snack, Ma? I'm starved as a skeleton."

"I know, like always. Your snack can be found in the banana peel and peanut butter jar. Think you can take it from there?"

"Nope."

"Well, I think maybe you can. And please don't throw away the bruised part unless it's awful bad."

"How come you're all lying down like that?"

"Cause I got very mad at J. Norris Simpson today, and it wiped me out. I can't abide that man, I can't."

"Can you abide Sebastian?"

"Squint and Scrawny, the comedy team."

"What?"

"Yeah, I can abide Sebastian. I think he's sort of pathetic, though. You know what that means?"

"Nope."

"Oh well, it doesn't matter. Can you abide him? You know what 'abide' means, don't you? Good for you, you're a smart little kid."

"Yeah, I can abide him, but sometimes he's a little meaner than you."

"What's mean about him?"

"I don't know."

"He's just very odd, Meadow. But if he ever does anything mean to you, be sure to tell me. And listen, if J. Norris ever, ever bothers you, come straight to me."

"He doesn't."

"Good. He better not."

"You know what Antlers does, though? It's so yucky. He hurts frogs."

"I don't doubt it at all. Are you finished talking about Ian? You're hopping in your talk like a little frog yourself."

Meadow solemnly finished her banana. The child seemed exceptionally still, transfixed, and pale.

"He just eats their arms and legs, but not the rest," she continued, wiping sticky fingers on her cutoffs. "He doesn't even kill them, he just eats off their arms and their legs, and they look *horrible*, Ma."

Hannah sat up on the bed.

"Meadow, Antlers doesn't know any better. He doesn't mean to be bad, he's just eating the part that tastes good. He doesn't know he's making the frog suffer." Meadow gave her a bleak look but didn't answer.

"Baby, yucky things happen to animals very often in this world. Did you know that someone killed J. Norris' horse?"

Meadow shook her head no. Her composure was beginning to crumble.

"Now *that* was evil, Meadow. Some fool with a gun destroyed an innocent animal for the heck of it. I hate guns. Guns aren't the same as nature."

Meadow crawled onto the bed, burying her head in Hannah's lap, making her mother glad she had a lap to offer.

"Meadow, don't cry. What's the matter, Goose? There's nothing to cry about. Did I say something I shouldn't have?"

"I'm scared," she whimpered.

"Because the horse got shot?"

"I don't know."

"Well, try to know. Try to think of one particular thing you're scared of."

Meadow gave a last muffled sob and seemed to redirect her energies from tears to thought. Hannah stroked her daughter's silken curls. "Tell me one thing, then we'll talk about it."

"Horses."

"You're afraid of horses? Just plain old horses?"

"Uh huh. Mr. Simpson's horses. When I'm down in the barn, they breathe on me."

"How do you mean, they breathe on you?"

Meadow made a snorting sound through her nose and did a good imitation of a bobbing horse's head.

"Oh, I know what you mean. Horses breathe funny, don't they? All noisy and hot. But they only snuffle around like that because they're smelling you for food. They stay in their stalls, don't they?"

Meadow nodded yes.

"Well, then, if you don't get too close, you're safe. Next time a horse snorts at you, look him straight in the eye and tell him to give you a whinny because he's your Dappled Gray Darling!"

"I can't say hard things like that. I'll just call him Darling. Then he'll be my friend."

"That's the way to go. Know what? He's already your friend because you don't walk around with a gun and shoot at him for the fun of it. He knows you're one of the good guys."

Hannah gave her daughter a searching look. “You wanna take a pancake down to the road tomorrow? I bet horses love pancakes.”

Meadow smiled wanly.

“Would you like that?”

“Uh huh. That way he’ll *know* I’m a good guy.”

8.

Sebastian's knock sent Hannah flying for the door. "Come in, come in, I was hoping you'd show up, I was lying here dying to see you! You'll never guess what's been happening around here, don't even try."

At this greeting Ian took one step backward before she grabbed his arm and pulled him over the threshold. "I can't get it off my mind. I mean, the more I think about it, the worse it gets. I seem to float around in this enormous, idiotic limbo. Is there such a word as 'limbotic'? That's what yesterday was." She stood before him, her hair a wild, tangled heap, wearing a pink nylon gown, which had been shortened with scissors one steamy night.

"I just got here," he said politely. "You're hurting my arm."

"Oh, I'm sorry."

"That's quite all right, Hannah, but let it go." He gently broke her grip himself.

"If I sound hysterical, I'm not, it's just that I'm so happy you're here, Ian, because I have got to talk to someone about J. Norris Simpson. I've been keeping this all to myself, but it's more than I can handle. That man is driving me over the edge! I *hate* him. Don't just stand there, Sebastian." She neatly kicked the door shut, grabbing at and missing his wrist. "If I ever needed a friend, it's right now. I'm about to reveal my inner life. What's the matter?"

"You keep assaulting me."

"All I wanna do is talk!"

"Hannah, give me time to adjust. I'm not used to seeing you so déshabillé." He gestured at her twice, indicating first her head, then her torso.

"My nightgown?"

"And your hair."

"So what? Haven't you ever seen your mother or your sister in her nightgown? I'm covered up. For pity's sake, I forgot to brush my hair!"

"Please don't get upset."

"I *am* upset! I'm coming completely unglued! My landlord is stalking me. Stalking, I tell you. Only he won't make his move. Yesterday he *almost* did, but then he didn't."

"What exactly do you mean? Be more specific."

"I don't know what I mean."

"What does he do?"

"He doesn't do anything, that's the part I can't stand!" Her voice rose to the next thing under a shriek. "But I can tell that I, that I, *affect* him. He comes around all the time, and he's very *affected* and cagey. Yesterday was different, I'll admit, but it wasn't any better because he was full of insinuations."

"Be more specific!"

"That I run a whorehouse single-handed or something!"

"Calm down, Hannah, lower your voice. You're making *me* a nervous wreck. What do you say we have ten minutes of total silence before we continue this conversation?"

The idea distracted her. "Meditation," she said. "That's a good idea. You wanna cushion?"

He had already taken a half-lotus position on the floor and shut his eyes, so she did a Girl Scout version of the same thing. Almost immediately, she felt more calm. They sat in silence for some time, until he signaled by rapping the floor with his knuckle. When she glanced at him, he was staring back uncertainly.

"You can relax," she said, "I feel better. Spiritual as a yellow tomcat. Thank goodness you came! This is the sixth time, I've been counting."

"My pleasure. Full-lotus is better, but I'm not limber enough yet. You sit like a child."

"Sebastian, could I ask you to do something for me? It's not the most celestial token of friendship, but it would mean a lot."

"I seem to recall making an offer that was rejected." He gave her a thin, wicked smile, which she overlooked.

"Would you sleep here tonight? Between J. Norris and his dead horse, I could use a little company. I'm afraid someone might come prowling after another animal. If I heard even one shot, I'd go through the roof."

"To what dead horse do you so sincerely refer?" The way he said it told her he'd stay. He was thinking about it, though. After all, he'd only volunteered to do some chores.

"I haven't had a chance to tell you. Someone shot my landlord's horse."

"Outside this house?"

"No, but I'm still jittery, and I don't want Meadow to know it. She depends on me. She thinks I'm never scared, so I gotta keep up appearances."

"To tell you the truth, I'd much prefer to see you afternoons and walk back mornings. My friggin' zookeeper has it in for me. Everyone else can keep their own hours, but if I'm not in every work party, every day, if I so much as, as – "

"Great. That's a big relief. How about coffee?"

"Hannah, how many times have I told you I don't drink coffee? I'm allergic to it."

"Hundreds. I keep forgetting. You want some tea?"

"Please."

"Maybe I should spruce up?"

He smiled noncommittally, blushing till his neck was red. Looking at it made her remember he'd left that boring red shirt at home again. She thought the blue one he'd finally switched to was much more suave.

"That shirt matches your eyes."

He continued to blush.

"This pink, on the other hand, does not match my eyes."

"No, I can't say that it does."

"If I were a rabbit, it might."

"Hannah," he pleaded.

"Better an innocent bunny than a good-time woman."

"You resemble one more than the other."

"Don't be sassy."

Taking a hairbrush from a small basket hanging on a nail, she began working at the thick, dark mass of hair. "You know, brother-on-the-road, I haven't appreciated you enough. But I'm gonna change. And just to show you how much I'm gonna change, I'll sing you a little song about that villain Sam McGee – no, I mean that villain, J. Norris McGee." Without warning, she held the hairbrush to her mouth as though it were a microphone.

"Put that down. I don't think you're funny."

"Don't worry, I'm just kidding. I have a right to be weird, though, same as you. All Americans have an equal right. By the way, did you know you're practically sitting on his POSTED: KEEP OUT sign? Ian, let me tell you a long, sad story." She glided toward the couch and sat down beside him.

"Hannah, I'll be honest, I can't stand your mood."

"Neither can I, but there it is." His chastisement left her on the verge of tears.

"I thought you were all grown up now," he said impatiently.

"Only on occasion, and this isn't one of them. Ian, what am I gonna do about my landlord?"

"I don't know! I have so many problems of my own, I can't solve yours. I wish you wouldn't ask me things like that."

"It's okay for you to lean on me, but not the other way around?"

Sebastian didn't say anything. Neither did Hannah. They sat together on the couch, uncomfortably still, waiting on the other one and on the mood – uniting or not – however long it took to crystallize.

"We don't know each other very well, do we?" she commented. He shook his head no.

Hannah cleared her throat theatrically. "Let's change the subject. Did you know my landlord suspects you of shooting his horse?"

"Me? How could he think I did it? How does he even know who I am?"

"That's a good question. He must have seen you walking over here. The cows in that pasture you walk through are his."

"Why would I shoot his horse?"

"You hippies would just as soon shoot a horse as set on one."

"I'm not a hippie. I don't even have long hair."

Hannah nodded. "If you're different, you're a hippie. I know it's nonsense."

"A couple of days ago, one of Justin's horses was shot. I heard him say the vet took a 12-gauge slug from its head."

"Who's Justin?"

"He owns the property – Mr. Altruistic Zookeeper, a real hard ass. But I must say, no one gets away with shooting his horses. He found out who did it and drove the unfortunate to the county jail complex himself. Grabbed him in front of Mitchell's store."

"Whodunit?" asked Hannah, fascinated by the tremors rippling through Ian's jaw.

"Some local yokel. A fifteen-year-old who went on a rampage because no one lets him use their land to hunt squirrels or possums, whatever people hunt this time of year. I wasn't informed of all the details. No one tells me anything because they know I'm about to leave."

"Seriously?" She watched the color drain from his face, from his neck, like serum from a bottle; so rapid was the transformation, she feared he would faint, but instead he grew more energetic, sweeping his arm across the room as though clearing debris.

"Who needs their help? I can always come here."

"My gosh, Ian, don't think that. I mean, what about the work crew?"

"Let's put it this way," he said, breathing deeply to steady himself. "They were the ones who invited me to come." He turned to look at Hannah. "I am often *invited* to come, but not in a way I can count on."

"They're your friends."

"The initiative was all theirs. The six-month trial period was their idea too, but I made it through that, so what are they waiting for? When I walk into a room, they change the subject. Of course, it's plain they discuss it, for all the good it does me. Whatever they decide, that's the name of the game. But they're not as close to checkmate as they think."

She could feel him begin to shake in earnest. This was the last thing she expected. It sounded like he thought they were seriously conniving against him.

"Wherever I go, I have to cry to the heavens I'm weird, like a leper ringing his bell. That's the only protection I have! It wasn't my plan to leave, but in a place like that, Hannah, a leper has no rights, you just wait till they've had enough of you." He took another long shuddering breath that sounded like a sob, but wasn't. His face was angry and strained, the color of old paste.

"You know what I think? They won't be satisfied till they wipe out every *trace* of my stay there, that's what it comes down to. But you can't do that, Hannah. The forces of the universe will undermine their effort. You can't escape karma. It's against God's will to try to wipe out every trace of any human being."

He took both her hands, holding them lightly, as though they were precious ornaments. All at once he seemed sure of his ground, serenely hoping to share the truth with a fellow seeker. "We both know God's will is simple."

"Sebastian, that doesn't sound ... for heaven's sake." She tried to be deferential because it was clear no other approach would work. "I can't believe they want to wipe out every trace of you. That doesn't seem right at all." How did he ever get that idea?

"It's not right, Hannah, and they won't succeed, so everything I've said is theoretical. What I can't escape from is their desire. See, it's the *desire* to cancel me out that I sense."

"Sebastian, I am positive you misunderstand what's going on. They're human beings, too, aren't they? No one wants to cancel out anyone else." She thought of Hitler. "I mean, it's possible, Sebastian, but that doesn't make it true."

Finally he began to cry softly, hopeless sobs. He was almost bent double in his pain, wrenching her hands now as though they weren't so precious after all. He was such a mercurial person.

Minutes went by before she realized he was calm again, though she had no idea what he was thinking or feeling.

"Sebastian?" She was relieved when he raised his head and looked at her in the normal way. Perhaps he was faintly posed, but that was normal enough for him.

"Are you okay?"

"I'm fine, Hannah. It was good of you to try and help me. The mother in you is very strong. Now tell me why your landlord thinks I shot his horse."

"Ian, I can't adjust that fast. Simpson and his dead horse seem pretty unreal at the moment."

"Why's that? When I walked in, you were coming 'unglued'."

"Well, more recently than that, you were too, and it was rather intense. Are you sure you're going to be all right?"

"I'll make it." He sounded wary.

"Sebastian, I'm worried about you."

"You still have your nightgown on."

"What's that got to do with your situation?"

"Hannah, have you ever wanted to kiss me?"

She took it in stride. "I suppose the idea has crossed my mind. It usually does."

"Would kissing a sister-on-the-road be considered incest?"

"I'm glad to see you've got your sense of humor back."

This was a poor occasion to reject his affection, and an equally poor occasion for romance. Surely this couldn't be a romantic request, not really. It had to be a silly whim, which she should go along with.

"Okay, let's kiss. Nothing fancy. You go first."

Sebastian leaned toward her and planted a brief, soft kiss on her lips. Then he moved so he was closer and held her very competently, much to her surprise.

"You must have had a girlfriend before."

"I haven't. What about you? Have you had any boyfriends?"

Hannah broke into an exhausted laugh. "I'm a *bona fide* mother, remember?" She expected him to blush, and perhaps he did, but he held her so close she couldn't see his face.

9.

"Make sure he keeps his eyes closed," cautioned Meadow, hugging a box of graham crackers.

"Ian, I hope you know cheating will get you nowhere."

"I'm not interested enough to cheat. How long do I have to lie here? I'm about to sneeze. Maybe you should sweep."

"That would make it worse, believe me. Meadow, gimme that kerchief. We'll blindfold this cheater."

Hannah kept her hand on Ian's chest to discourage him from sitting up. As an after-supper form of entertainment, this game wasn't much, but it was the sort of thing she and Meadow did after dark.

"There we go. Okay, the time has come to open your mouth. Not too wide, we don't want to choke you. That's good. Now, Meadow, feed him a little piece of *coconut*."

"Your coconut sounds like crackers." He chewed it. "Tastes like a graham cracker to me."

"No it doesn't," said Meadow. "It tastes like coconut if you play right."

"Concentrate, Sebastian. Meadow and I have discovered that almost everything tastes like coconut if you tell yourself it does."

"I'm not good at games. Besides, I'm not fond of coconut."

"You gotta let yourself go, Sebastian. Make an act of the will. Hey, Meadow, try one more thing."

The child reached into her pocket and pulled out an orange lifesaver. "This?"

"That might work."

"Never mind you two, I'm getting a stiff neck. This isn't the most exciting game I ever played."

"How do you like that?" Hannah faked an incredulous expression and looked at Meadow, whose own astonishment carried conviction. "He's not excited! Well, take off his blindfold. His taste bud chromosomes aren't the same as ours, some wiggly piece is missing. Now the only thing left to do is go to bed."

"Ah, Ma!"

"Nope, no arguing. The clock says I'm right. Good thing Ian wasn't having fun or you'd be too tired for school tomorrow. Get on your nightie and brush your teeth, Babe. I'll make up the bed and bring your pillow in. Ian, I hope you don't mind sleeping with no pillow. We only have two."

"If Meadow can do without her bed, I can do without her pillow."

"Well-spoken," said Hannah. Although she wanted him to stay, the thought of having him all night was now agitating. She didn't know if she'd be able to sleep.

All of a sudden Ian held a finger to his lips. "What was that? Did you hear it?" He cocked his head listening for something.

"What?" asked Meadow, immediately alarmed.

Hannah was sure she hadn't heard anything, but she'd been edgy all evening. If they weren't careful, the atmosphere would turn spooky.

"It's a new game, Meadow. All you have to do is tip your head to one side, and you can hear coconuts falling out of coconut trees. See, like this." She smiled reassuringly at her daughter. "See, just like this. Listen . . . plop, plop, plop."

"I'm glad I get to sleep in your bed."

"Me too."

"Where's Ian going?"

"I don't know. Where are you going, Ian?"

"Outside to water the flowers. It's a polite expression."

"In the dark?" said Meadow.

"He's peeing," Hannah informed her. "When he comes in, we'll go out." They were lucky to have someone out there testing the shadows for them. She pulled off a faded pink smock, which looked like a nightie, and reached for the morning's genuine pink nightie hanging on a nail. It didn't feel strange to wear a nightgown around him now. She decided that was progress, though toward what goal she wasn't sure.

Hannah wished she could sleep like Meadow: hot, heavy, fast. Her way was opposite: cold, light, slow. Yes sir: hold, tight, fro; fold, bite, woe. Yes sir: jold, dight ...

At the strum of his guitar, she opened her eyes and stared blankly into the darkness. The notes were soft, not even as loud as the cicadas whose mindless crescendos throbbed outside her window. "Listen to them," she told herself, "concentrate on the bugs." With her toes she kept time to outdoor rhythms. "Ignore him, ignore him, ignore him" she whispered.

I ain't nothing but a pun, hun
dee dee dum, bum bum
I ain't nothing but a gun, hun

You again.

dee dee dum, bum bum

Go away. I'm ignoring you.

You might as well take me for granite

Make him go away, God.

Old Man God's a stone – maybe granite, maybe quartz
'Bout as big as a rock or a tooth or a horny toad

"Sebastian?" Having moved to his doorway, she saw him jump. "Are you awake?"

"Now I am. What's wrong?"

"I can't get to sleep."

There was no answer unless it was the motionless outline of his body. "Could I lie down with you? Would you hold me like you did before?"

"All of a sudden today, I seem to be your favorite person."

"Wasn't it this morning you asked for a kiss?" She had turned to leave when he grabbed her nightgown and pulled her down beside him.

"Don't go."

"I don't see any reason not to."

"Because I don't want you to, Hannah. You just surprised me, that's all. I hate the sound of someone tiptoeing on a squeaky floor. I'll hold you."

Caught between reluctance and relief, she stretched out beside him with her head on his shoulder and her arm across his bare chest. He'd covered them with the sheet, and now she wondered if he were nude or not. She'd have to change her position to tell. This was amazing -- lying in bed with a man after so many years.

"You need to eat more. Your collarbone hurts to lie on."

"Don't then." He withdrew his arm.

"You *are* mad!"

He did not deny it.

"I'm going back in with Meadow."

"Do *you* like hearing you're too fat, too thin, too tall, too short? I know I'm underweight, people have told me that all my life."

"I'm sorry, Ian. I didn't mean to be critical. I was just teasing."

"You do too much of that. It gets on my nerves."

"You're probably right. I'm very sorry." This was awful. She felt like a fool, and what was worse, she planned on remaining a fool to avoid being ridiculed by the Mouth in there. Only he probably wasn't "in there." She closed her eyes to ascertain if any vagrant music was following her around, but it didn't seem to be.

Night was hard, always getting harder, and she didn't know why. Maybe besides God and a down jacket, she needed sex.

"You know, I'm not really promiscuous. I haven't been in bed with a man for seven years."

"I told you we were a lot alike."

"Seven years ago, you were twelve."

"What happened to Meadow's father?"

"I don't know. He took the elevator, I took the stairs, that was that." She paused. "I'm not trying to sound cute. That's just the way it was."

Antlers jumped onto the foot of the bed and came padding up their bodies with live whiskers and silver eyes. He kneaded the cover near their faces and purred loudly.

"That's something I meant to ask you. You and your nature names. Antlers? For a cat? What does it mean?"

"I dunno. My mother named him. I just liked the sound of it; who knows? I should ask her. It fits him, don't you think?"

He pushed the cat onto the floor with a thud.

"Yep," said Hannah, "a good-old one night stand. He was a great guy. That night was the last time I had sex, the very last time."

"You didn't even know her father?"

"Well, I sorta knew him. I'd been dancing with him all evening." Hannah interpreted his silence as disapproval.

"I was a ba-ad woman, Sebastian, but now I've reformed. Now I'm your model mother and sister-on-the-road."

"Hannah, what are we doing in bed together?"

"We're talking. You're distracting me from bad dreams. You don't know it, but I have these Western nightmares. They're not *quite* the same as nightmares though."

He turned on his side and put a tentative hand on her breast. "Shh," he said.

"Do you want to make love?" she asked.

"I think not."

"You think not?" His hand was much less tentative now, confusing her. "Don't you like women?"

"I'm not called to relate to bodies of either sex. No, don't laugh. Go back to Meadow if you're going to laugh."

"Then why don't you keep your hand to yourself, and we'll only talk. If you don't want to make love, don't be sexual."

"You're the one who started all this," he snapped, moving his hand to the other breast. By now she knew he had his shorts on. She could also tell he was fully aroused.

"Well, *you're* the one who just raised the question of what we're doing in bed together. Let me tell you, brother, it's suddenly clear we're not just talking about bad dreams. I'm experienced enough to know." She turned on her side, pulling herself towards him, and began to kiss him on the mouth. He responded urgently enough to suit her.

"You're a whore, Hannah, you're a shameless hooker." His voice shook with eagerness.

Abruptly, she stopped kissing him and pulled away. "I am not," she said indignantly. "I most certainly am not." It was so dark she couldn't see his expression, but his breathing was ragged, almost a rattle. "Are you called to relate to bodies or not?" she demanded.

"Maybe to your body."

"I don't think so," she said, and went back in to Meadow whose breathing was sweet and reassuring. It seemed like hours before she fell asleep.

Hannah was still insulted the next morning.

It had rained during the night, ushering in a day that was fine and cool, with air that smelled somehow innocent. That smell would have gotten her off to a good start, but the thought of last night swung her back to the soft-boiled egg she had cracked open on Meadow's plate. It carried a pungent odor, worthy of blame. How could anyone eat sulfur first thing in the morning? All she wanted for hours was coffee.

"I wonder why bugs don't drown?" mumbled Hannah, who had left the table and was idly looking out the front door.

"Aren't there any left?" asked Meadow anxiously.

"Oh, I'm sure there are. I'm not looking for bugs, I'm just standing here looking out. Ian sleeps late, doesn't he?"

"He's awake. I saw him when I got my clothes."

"What's he doing?"

"Sitting on the floor with his eyes closed."

"That's good. He's meditating."

"He looks funny."

"God probably wouldn't think so. Uh oh, is that the bus? You better hurry, Mouse."

"I gotta go. Today's Friday, cupcake day!"

"You haven't brushed your teeth, Meadow."

"I'll miss the bus, Ma!"

"Okay! Go! *Go* out in the world with unbrushed teeth to eat rotten cupcakes!"

"They don't look rotten to God!" She giggled at her own wit. "Bye, Ma."

"God's only as big as a tooth anyway," muttered her mother, suddenly depressed. It wouldn't do to be insulted. She needed a friend. "Maybe God's a fang." She poured herself another cup of coffee, the only luxury it never occurred to her to give up.

Antlers rubbed against her leg. "You don't love me, you're just hungry."

"You don't love me either," said Sebastian, quite seriously. He entered the room fully dressed, buttoned at the neck and the wrists. He seemed to have gotten thinner in twenty-four hours.

"I was talking to the cat."

He didn't seem to take it in, so she stood up and announced that the hussy wasn't in her nightgown, and she'd finally brushed her hair. His wince brought her to her senses.

"Ian, ignore that last remark. I want to apologize. I'm ashamed of myself, and, you know, about last night. I didn't move down here to wander *on* the beaten path."

"Hannah …."

She waited for him to make his apology, the one that would help extinguish her tongue for the rest of the day. When he did speak, he sounded hoarse, and his eyes were different, as though he'd successfully fought off sleep for days.

"I'm going now. But I'll be back tonight."

"That's not necessary, Sebastian. I think I'm over my attack of nerves. Simpson's not a monster, after all. My problem with him is I just can't read him, you know? We're culturally different, we don't understand each other's ways. I'm sure I don't need a bodyguard for heaven's sake. You come back a few days from now and we'll dig sweet potatoes, if we can locate the patch."

"It might be late, but I'm coming."

"Don't do that. We'll act out some stupid charade. Look, Sebastian, you were right. You're not called to 'relate to bodies.' Me neither. Can't you see we're both after something else? If we're supposed to do anything, it's encourage each other to be alone."

"We have to talk, but there's no time now. I've got to go. But I understand more than you think. You *are* the one I've been looking for, Hannah; it's just that I've been slow to trust you. When you live in a world of traps, you have to be careful. Justin's girlfriend was a trap I avoided. You've got to remember, I've had to be on guard."

"Sebastian," she shook her head in dismay, "don't complicate the uncomplicated. We're just friends."

He walked over to her and before she had time to react, kissed her cordially on the lips.

"Give me a break," he said. "I'm new at this."

Poignantly, she shook her head no. She could feel her stomach begin to churn as he ducked out the door. Why was the world trying to complicate itself again? Was there no reward for following reason?

After she forced down some oatmeal, she would nail that KEEP OUT sign to the tree, and while she pounded it on, she'd consider ways to encourage a troubled young man's chastity. That was the virtuous thing to do; it would also keep his weirdness in check and save her a friend, which she needed.

In any event, Cowboy was her toughest entanglement, not Sebastian, or even Simpson. She couldn't say he's troubled, or spout that hogwash about being culturally different and not understanding one another's ways. In fact, the more she thought about Cowboy, the more she knew there were no excuses for him at all, or for the boundaries he crossed. She knew he was *her*, and she desperately prayed she would prevail again him.

10.

Simpson turned up the slope while Hannah was resting in her doorway. An afternoon sun was in her face making it hard to watch his progress up the hill, but she had no interest in it anyway, preferring to look elsewhere as long as she could.

She let her gaze travel along the ground in the direction of the garden, which was out of sight around the house. After hours of attention, it had rows again; she knew where to find her overripe squash or the sweet potatoes and, as a result, she couldn't keep her eyes from traveling back in that direction like ants on a trail of sugar.

Temporary peace with nature and blistered hands had almost led her to undress for a swim, but the sound of his pickup spoiled that idea. She'd never gone in the pond. It didn't look healthy. Recently, though, she'd been feeling the calm pull of some dim, ignoble fate, and it occurred to her that dying the color of a pumpkin from hepatitis might be her earthly destiny. All the same, Simpson was coming. He was destiny enough for one morning.

She watched him only at the last moment, as he pulled to a stop about thirty-six inches from her still unjaundiced, mortal flesh. "Whatever happens, don't get mad," she told herself, "after you've worked your fingers to the bone getting calm."

She squinted up at him with ant-like patience, trying to imagine his green pickup as a large, growing, rooted object. It didn't work.

"Well, well, well, well, well," she said, conscious of her failure, "if it isn't good old J. Norris." The sun wasn't in *his* eyes, but he blinked as though it were.

"Good morning, Hannah. Though I reckon it ain't morning." It was a pleasant surprise that he didn't get out of his truck.

"The traditional term is afternoon."

"I like red, don't matter who it's on."

"Thanks," she said, glancing down at her red peasant blouse with a look that implied he had rotten taste. Then she pointed to the tree. "See there? I put your sign up so you can quit worrying about trespassers and hopefully sleep nights."

"Thank you, Hannah. It don't look bad. A little crooked, but mighty official. Now you make sure that beau of yours lays his eyes on it."

"Which beau do you mean?" she asked archly. "Oh, the one that killed your horse? Yeah, I showed him, and he was so impressed, he decided to stop shooting horses and definitely to quit me as his friend. An effective sign, J. Norris."

"Now Hannah, don't go jumping the gun again. I didn't say nothing about my horse. Fact of the matter is, I know who done it."

"Found him, huh?"

"The law got to him without no help from me, but that don't mean I set back in my chair and waited for the newspaper to come out with his name." He shook his head as though it were hard to understand. "Seems like he killed hisself more than one horse, though I don't know why he had to go and pick mine. I've known his Daddy for years."

"I heard the news that he wasn't a hippie."

"I reckon you want me to eat my words. Well, I'll admit it. I was dead wrong on that score. It wasn't no hippie."

"So tell me if you can, what does that sign have to do with one male person Meadow and I have gotten acquainted with?"

"He's got no business on my property. I don't go for all that dope smoking and I hope you don't either. Next thing I know, he'll be growing it here." He stayed in his truck.

"I don't smoke anything stronger than coffee, and he doesn't even do that. Can't you get it through your head he's not a hippie, whatever that is? He's just an oddball friend. But he's not such an oddball that he'll stop coming to see me because of a KEEP OUT sign. Give it fifteen seconds of thought J. Norris and you'll blush at yourself."

Simpson leaned his head on the steering wheel and closed his eyes.

"Good Lord, he *is* giving it fifteen seconds of thought," she concluded, but then he raised his head again and looked at her with the reddest rimmed eyes she had ever seen.

"The world goes on whether you blush at yourself, or hate yourself, or just plain give up. There's nothing you can tell me about blushing I ain't known for years. But you ain't known *me* for years, and how I promised myself I wouldn't ever rent to certain kinds again. It brings nothing but hardship all around." He heaved a sigh that covered the past and brought him back to Hannah.

"If you ain't forgot, I'll remind you. When you moved in here, I told you in plain words how I felt about loose living. I wouldn't have rented you this place – my grandmother lived here when she was a girl, you know that? – if I'd known you was the kind to carry on with men. I figured I was taking a chance, see, owing to how you're a right attractive gal, but these things aren't so easy to ...."

"Mr. Simpson, I don't carry on with men! I have lived here for months, and you are practically the only man I've even spoken to. You couldn't have found anyone who carried on less than me and my daughter. And it's none of your business anyway!"

"Look a-here," he said, in a voice thick with supplication, "it ain't convincing to tell me what goes on in this house ain't got something to do with me. I'm legally responsible for this property. And I'll be downright frank with you. You can't tell me you don't carry on with men because I've seen that young baldy coming and going with my own eyes. Hell, I saw the kid a few hours ago walking out that doorway. It don't do to deny something as plain as day. I'm sorry to say it in so many words."

"You want me to explain that? It goes against all my principles, but I will, so you can get past this troublesome obsession you seem to have."

Simpson waited unhappily for her explanation.

"That's someone I've only known for a month, six weeks at most. He lives over the ridge and has visited a number of times since

I met him. Last night I asked him to spend the night with Meadow and me because I was afraid. Gun-toting horse killers happen to make me nervous. But that 'young baldy' is not a trespasser or a boyfriend. He didn't disgrace me, or you, or your precious property. He just slept in Meadow's room. Now, to you that may seem scandalous, but that's the difference in our ages. Plus, we're different culturally, if you know what I mean."

Simpson maintained his glum expression.

"Have we settled that point?" she asked, willing to go on if necessary.

His answer was ready; she suspected he'd driven up the slope with it. "It don't seem right for a woman like you to live alone here," he replied. "You're a fine mother to Meadow, and I can't see no real harm in what you're doing living so poor, though I can't say I understand it neither. But I don't see no real harm in it if you take good care of your daughter, which I've always said you do. But you're a heavy temptation to others, Hannah, and that don't seem right."

"There aren't any others out here! Who am I a heavy temptation to, J. Norris? Is it you? Have I ever led you on in any way?"

"No, Hannah, I can't say you have. And when I was able, I done you what service I could, both Ma and me. I don't think it's likely you have any cause to complain about the way we've treated you neither."

"You've done a lot for me, that's for sure. And I guess I don't have any cause to complain so long as you don't expect me to get your approval on the people I see."

"I don't expect nothing," he informed her rather hopelessly, "except for you to be decent and watch out for yourself and that girl of yours. There's things in this world you don't understand, but it's beyond me to explain them." He turned on the ignition, so she knew he didn't expect a reply, not with him racing the engine like that. She turned away and waited for the sounds of his leaving to fade, but when they reversed themselves and began to grow, she swung around only to see him backing up the slope with his head out the window.

"Round two," she thought, going to meet him. She had not prepared herself to find him crying. Though he was calm enough, his cheeks were covered with tears that rolled in pale sheets off the fleshy planes of his face. She had never seen such quantity of tears. They had actually deepened the green on the side of his cab.

What was she supposed to do? Why didn't he drive straight down the hill with all his fluids to his wife? Why was he always, ever since she came here, turning back in her direction?

Unable to meet her gaze, he turned the key to "off" and reached into his pocket for a handkerchief with which to mop his eyes. He looked like a picture of dejection as he stared into the distance; that very aspect, portrait of an unhappy farmer, distanced Hannah from her anger. In a voice flat as paper she said, "Mr. Simpson, have I hurt your feelings?"

"No, it ain't that."

"What is it then?"

"Hannah, there's something you don't understand about me, something only the Lord knows about so far."

"That's true of everyone."

"Yes, but this particular thing is a deal more than that. It's something about me you might hate me for if you was the hating kind, which you ain't."

"Oh yes I am."

"Well, I ain't no judge of that," he said, wiping his nose before he put the handkerchief back in his pocket.

"You talk like you're a Dr. Jekyll and Mr. Hyde." Her voice held a hint of disbelief she put there out of politeness. The Hyde in him had been reducing her to shreds for months now.

He kept watching whatever lay beyond the windshield. "Maybe you hit the nail on the head. If you knew what I genuinely am, you wouldn't want to rent from me. You'd take that girl of yours and run away. I backed up the hill just to tell you that, Hannah, to tell you it'd be a smart thing for you to do, to leave without things going no further. This house of mine ain't no place for a fine looking woman from somewheres else to settle down."

It was a speech that awed her. No one had ever said anything even remotely like that to her before.

"Are you ... you aren't are you? I mean, sometimes I've been afraid you might want to hurt -- "

"I'm not a murderer if that's what you're getting at. I'm a peaceable man as far as that goes."

"Are you a rapist?" She held her breath in case he said the preposterous, "I surely am and you are my next victim." What was this, Little Red Riding Hood? Mr. Simpson, What Big Eyes You Have?

"Honey," he said softly, and his eyes did indeed glisten and look magnified, though she only saw them from the side, "if you get attacked, it'll most likely be them hippies over the ridge. That boyfriend of yours, he's nice and weak looking, but I reckon you could stir him up plenty and get yourself a proper rapist if that's the terror that draws you. I'm too old-fashioned for wildness like that. But right this minute I'm trying to warn you about *myself*, like I was speaking for a friend you don't know. The idea just come to me as I was driving off, and I give in to it, thinking maybe to undo some of the misery by telling you this. "

"If you're not a murderer or a rapist, are you a kidnapper or do you molest children or …." This whole thing was becoming more outlandish. How many perverse habits were there, and how long did she have to think up the right one? Simpson, too, seemed to realize the foolishness of this line of questioning.

"I just come to tell you, listen! You'd be better off to get the hell out of here!" The words splattered her like blood. Then he put the truck in gear, refocused his faraway stare and roared down the slope with a face less calm, but dry at last.

Hannah stood where she was, too shaky and disturbed to do anything more than follow his jolting progress down to the road. She should load up the car and leave when Meadow got home from school. Only she didn't have a car, except that junk heap down near the gully, and it wouldn't do her a damn bit of good to try to escape in that.

Pang, pang, you're dead! Paaaaang, paaaaang

The Cowboy hooted at her merrily as he pulled the trigger; she could have strangled him, but that – she supposed – would only be suicide.

11.

"Ma, you're not listening."

"Yes, I am. You just said, um, that Kenny was a big booger."

"That was a long time ago."

"What did I miss?"

"I told you *two times* that Animal Rummy is only for babies, and all you said was don't worry about it." Meadow folded her hand and laid it on the table. "Please do I have to play cards anymore?"

"Of course you don't," said Hannah, tossing her pair of camels across the room, "not if it's only for babies. Anyway, I'm bored to tears too."

"Me no see-um," said Meadow, who was wearing a feathered Indian Chief hat, in tribute to her Indian ancestors, none of whom had names they knew.

"There they are," said her mother, pulling her eyelid down to exhibit her collection of tears.

"You got red eyes just like Mr. Simpson. What do mine look like?" Meadow pulled her own eyelid down for inspection.

"It looks bored in there."

"Oh it is, it is," said Meadow in a staged voice. "Let's sing instead!"

"Naw, let's eat cinnamon toast," her mother replied.

"Let's dress up and dance around a bonfire!" countered Meadow.

"Naw, let's not."

"What's wrong? Are you mad at me?"

"Why on earth would I be mad at you? I hardly ever get mad at you."

"I dunno," said Meadow.

"Where are you going?"

"To bed."

"Listen, Goose, I'm not mad, not a bit! You don't have to go to bed for fifteen more minutes. Don't you want some cinnamon toast?"

"Uh-uh, I'm tired. I wanna go to bed."

"Come here and let me feel your forehead." With cheerless inconsonance, Meadow did as she was told.

"You're not hot."

"I'm *tired*!" she repeated, in the beginning of real distress.

"Okay, okay, I got the message. Gimme a kiss and have sweet dreams because you're a good little girl who deserves them." They exchanged a loud smack, then a slight smile that began and ended around the eyes with the mouth being incidental.

After her daughter left the room, Hannah felt more free to consider her latest idea, stealing a car. "Be serious," she told herself, but the discipline involved seemed enormous.

Inertia had settled on her like motion sickness, leaving her even less inclined to stir up serious thought. Certainly she was going to leave, but how to accomplish it? And where to go? These kinds of questions felt like fingers she refused to stick down her throat at this hour. Even if she could finally vomit up some logical answers, there was no hope for getting out tonight.

She looked up from the floor when she heard the doorknob jiggle. "That's not the wind," she thought, watching the knob rotate, listening to its soft, non-protesting click. Dreamily she wondered why she hadn't locked the door. Now she had to defend them both. First she had to find the bat. She stood up, but it was too late.

Sebastian walked in with a black canvas pack thrown over his shoulder. She remembered in a flash that she was safe; she hadn't convinced him to sleep in his own bed. She lived in a world of reinforcements!

"Ian, you've come to my rescue in the nick of time!"

"After this morning, I didn't expect a hero's welcome. You and I can't seem to get our signals straight." He looked haggard.

"You look terrible," she said, giving it no thought, and watched his eyes warn her away from that line of comment.

"I'm thirsty, that's all. How about a drink?"

"Certainly, darling." It never ceased to amaze her, the stupid things she said. She filled a quart jar with water and handed it to him without ice. The evening was cool. In the last few days the summer's haze had cleared considerably, and earlier dusk had taken its place in the opaque order of things. The crickets had been going strong for hours.

"You knew I'd be here. You've been on my mind, to say the least, all day."

She felt almost guilty. By afternoon, he'd been as absent from her own thoughts as Simpson was present. Ian was not the man she expected to confront.

"Yes, it's been quite a day," she offered, hoping it was enough to slide by. "Sit down. That pack looks heavy. What on earth is in it?"

"Where's Meadow?"

"In bed."

He looked over at the couch, which was not pulled out yet, then back at Hannah. It occurred to her that he had nowhere to sleep except on the floor or with her. He would read that as an intentional move on her part. She laughed nervously, wondering at her own ineptitude.

"I didn't mean to thicken the plot. It was an accident."

With his usual tremulous, self-important air, he set his pack on the floor. He reminded her of something slight. A piece of straw. The one you find driven through a telephone pole after a tornado.

Giving way to impulse, she tried to recall what his bare chest looked like. Only the bony feel of his body had stayed with her, not its image. He couldn't have hair on his chest or she'd remember it against her cheek. She advised herself to think about something else, since she had wisely renounced pleasures of the flesh. It would be better to try and decide why he continued to stand there when she'd invited him to sit.

"Take a seat, Ian. We've got lots of time to figure out the sleeping arrangements. I mean, I'm assuming sex is the last thing on both our minds. You should have heard me tell Simpson how platonic we are."

"Where'd you meet *him*?"

"He came again like he always does. He took it upon himself to warn me, that's why I was so glad to see you. He -- "

"What made you discuss our private relationship with him?"

"He challenged me on it! He saw you leave this morning and decided that meant I fool around or something. So I just explained the whole thing, how I asked you to stay because I was scared, and how you slept in Meadow's room."

"You didn't mention you slept there too?"

"It just so happens I didn't sleep there. I lay down with you for awhile and after an unfortunate conversation, returned to my own room and slept in my own bed."

"Hannah," he said, his voice a soft accusation.

"Look, I refuse to admit to charges of loose living because I talked to you in a prone position. It's not sheer literal truth that matters."

"Why do you think I came back tonight?" And before she could reply, he answered his own question. "Because I have decided to take you up on your generous offer to help me decipher the facts of life."

His voice didn't sound too sure, but she searched his eyes and saw a bright, congealed look that was convincing proof of something more determined than the boyish quaver she took for granted.

"You're an unsteady soul. You don't know what you want."

"I do too." He met her eyes calmly

"Well, I didn't make an offer. And even if I had, I took it back twice, last night and this morning. But if you're worried about learning the facts of life, I didn't get the impression you needed teaching. All you lack is experience."

"At least that's clear! What's wrong with that?"

"*Nothing*, that's what I'm trying to tell you. You're fine just like you are. It suits you."

Sebastian moved toward her and held out his hand. It was a gentle, non-erotic gesture, one she couldn't refuse a friend, though the meaning of it escaped her. Then he bent his head and kissed what he held, finishing what he had started.

"It would never work, Ian, I really don't think it would. We're both too intense, we have too many idiosyncrasies, we've ..."

"We've been holding back. This morning in Meadow's room I reached an understanding of that. You might say it was given to me. There are spiritual ways to go about a physical relationship."

"Well, I agree, but I don't think last night was a sterling example."

"That was my fault, Hannah. I've always shied away from anything physical, always distrusted it. But the way you were, it opened up another dimension for me. I saw something utterly pure in you."

"No kidding."

"Don't give me that silly look. You're forever trying to weaken the truth with some sort of stupid derision. Can't you see you're only weakening yourself? I *saw* it in you, but not until this morning sitting beside your daughter's bed."

She stood there, perplexed. Too bad you couldn't bite statements to see if they were gold like those old codgers bit coins in the Westerns.

Once again he leaned down and kissed her hand, this time leaving his lips a longer time. She could feel his nervous energy like a current of electricity he had just plugged in above her fingers. She wondered if he would stoop to beg, and her sudden horror of that, of turning a beggar down, made her try to pull back her hand before it was too late.

"This is all too much to sort out," she pleaded, twisting her arm to free herself. "I've got to think about other things, believe me."

"Don't Hannah. Let me hold you. Remember how you asked the same of me? And I *did* hold you. Please. *Please*. You are the only woman I know who … I trust myself with. You are the only one it will go right with."

"*With whom it will go right*," she said, grasping at any poor joke to get away.

It was useless after all. Night was coming on. There was Simpson with his secret lowlife, the Cowboy with his ugly guitar, God with his disparaging blackness, and Sebastian with his need to be loved in the flesh by someone. It didn't matter who it was, as long as it was her.

"All right," she said, taking the thoroughfare of least resistance. "But after tonight, never again."

"Thank you, Hannah. I'm in earnest about that. Thank you."

"Now," he said, letting go of her hand to rub his temple, "We've got to go about this as dignified beings."

"Oh, the first move is simple because I'm only giving in if you'll tell me more about yourself. Unfold the couch and lie down. I intend to ask you a few pertinent questions."

He didn't look pleased. In fact, he was beginning to look rather ill. "I was thinking of something like massage Hannah, not interrogation."

"Please," she said, "lie down. Who's the mistress of this ceremony?"

He hesitated, but pulled the couch out and lay down with all his clothes on. Hannah lit two candles and removed her blue jeans without embarrassment. It looked like the beginning of a striptease, and would serve as one, but her real reason was domestic. Her blue jeans were grungy and she wanted to keep the sheet clean. She wouldn't say so though.

After tossing a blanket on the bed, and her one pillow, Hannah lay down herself. She saw Sebastian looking at her underpants as though at strange tropical fish. "Anymore, I don't believe in sexy underwear," she said, "but all the stores do."

"I don't believe in underwear at all," he retorted irritably. He was terribly flushed and looked cornered.

"Okay, numero uno. What's Justin like?"

"I'm not going into all that."

"Is he truly religious and dedicated and good?"

"Everyone thinks he is, but I'll tell you this, Hannah, they're all hypocrites of the first order. Can you believe it, they're rich? They're into Mammon. That's what I like about you."

"I'm a destitute of the first order."

"Don't waste my time with questions about any of them. I won't answer, so don't ask." He put his hand on her thigh, and its warmth felt good. As soon as she ran out of questions, they could give each other back rubs.

"What's your last name?"

"Dupré-White."

"Sebastian Dupré-White. I like it. If we ever got married, I could be Hannah Dupré White-Wolfe, couldn't I? When I braided my hair, everyone would think you had an Indian wife. Did you know I'm 25 percent Native American on my father's side? Maybe even 50 percent. What a sexy name you have." She fanned her dark hair across the pillow like a shadow, and he buried a hand in it. "Now that I know your surname, what does it matter?"

Moodily he shook his head no, he didn't want to talk about his name.

"Where are you from? How did you get to Kentucky?"

Sebastian looked even more cornered, but she couldn't take it seriously. There was nothing wrong with asking a man you were about to sleep with where he was from.

"Florida," he said, grudgingly.

"I'll bet your parents have a heavy investment in Mammon, am I right?"

He nodded yes and feigned an absent stare into space.

"What's the matter?" she asked, having a pretty good idea.

"You know I hate to answer personal questions, but you keep demanding I do it. The only relevant thing is that you and I are in bed, and you've offered to pursue a physical act with me in the interest of spiritual enlightenment."

"I didn't know I offered anything *that* grand."

"You didn't offer to muck around in the dirt."

"I didn't offer that either." She was beginning to feel angry so she stood up and walked over to the refrigerator. She looked inside, found herself staring at the cheese, decided she didn't want any cheese, and closed the door.

"Too bad I don't have any beer," she said. "I could use a drop too much."

His voice carried to her softly from the bed. "Take off your blouse, will you?"

"I suppose that's reasonable," she thought, and started to unbutton it. Capitulation wasn't much fun. The only reward for controlling her increasing annoyance was given to her vanity when she heard him draw in his breath after she removed her bra. It made her knees go ever so slightly weak.

"Now the panties, Hannah. Take them off with your back to me and turn around."

"You have quite developed tastes."

"Hardly. I've never done this before in my life and you know it. Hurry up now, I can't keep up with the images."

"What images?"

"The ones in my mind."

"Good God."

"Woman, you make me feel stronger," he half-whispered, "inside and out."

"You're gonna give me delusions of grandeur."

When she turned around, he got up from the bed and groaned as he unzipped his pants. He left his shorts on, but his erection was obvious, and in spite of herself, she wanted what she had known in the past, though it had little to do with him. She supposed her own emerging desire for penetration was nothing short of his images. All at once she was struck by the peculiarity and sadness of 'the night Sebastian lost his virginity'.

"Not too close, Hannah, stay right where you are."

"Listen, Sebastian, I don't wanna stay right where I am. I'm not some girlie on a stage." She walked back to the bed and lay down on top of him, out of the limelight. "And please, talk softer. I don't want to wake up Meadow."

"What can you show me?" he whispered.

"Nothing," she whispered back. "I don't have a very large repertoire."

"Your jokes sicken me, you know that?"

"Well, your images, whatever they are, sicken me."

He rolled himself on top of her and made several thrusts before she managed to push him back off.

"I'm changing my mind."

His response was obstinacy and a tighter grasp. She felt his words come spitting out into her hair, damp and jerky, "I'm going to have you whether you change your mind or not. One more man won't make that much difference, and this is something I need to do."

"The hell it is!" she almost shouted, anger rising in her like boiling sap as she found the strength to break loose. The room began to swim and take on a darker hue, or at least his face did. "Go find someone who charges, that's what you're really after! Maybe if you beg them, they'll give you a discount for being so spiritual."

She kept her distance from the bed -- naked, rooted instinctively in some adamantine stance that gave her courage, though it was far less safe than it looked since, after all, it was only Hannah standing in the middle of the floor undressed. But Sebastian lost his nerve. She had the aura of a legendary Sycamore, peeled and chalky, some looming natural object of hidden power.

"I hope you realize I'm stronger than you," he said haughtily, pulling his shorts back up. "If I wanted to, I could rape you, even as you make a spectacle of yourself. But you disgust me."

"Disgust plays an exciting role in your life, doesn't it?"

"Since when are you fit to read souls?"

"Mama, it's too noisy. I can't sleep." Meadow was standing in the doorway of her room, looking out with sleepy eyes that were beginning to register both surprise and fear.

Hannah wanted to drop dead, but — unable to achieve such command of the situation — she reached for a blanket instead, wrapped it around herself and, taking Meadow in hand, walked out the front door.

"This isn't easy to explain, but the main thing you need to know is that Sebastian and I are having a fight."

What about?" asked Meadow, her lower lip trembling as she tried to hold back tears.

"Well, first let's sit down. There's no good places to sit, so we'll just sit down any old where like Indians. Wanna come in my tent with me?" Hannah opened the blanket and Meadow crawled onto her lap after which Hannah rewound them as one.

"Our heads stick out the top of this tent," commented Meadow sorrowfully.

"I know. That's funny, isn't it?"

Sadly, she nodded yes.

"Okay, as I said, you walked in right when I was having a big fight with Ian, and I feel awful embarrassed and ashamed of myself."

"Was he hurting you?"

"No, he wasn't hurting me. He's not the kind to do that, so don't be afraid."

"I heard him say he was stronger."

"He was just bragging. Don't the boys at school ever do that? I bet that big booger, Kenny, says all sorts of things."

"Yep. He's always saying how strong he is."

"I thought so."

"Ma, why do you guys have your clothes off?"

"Ian's got his underpants on. As a matter of fact, I was just about to get dressed when you walked in."

"Were you hot?"

"Uh huh."

"Is Ian still our friend?"

"Sure. You wanna ask him?" Meadow nodded, brightening a little. "Well, go pop your head inside our door and do it," said Hannah, making a hole in the tent so Meadow could leave. She heard the question when it was asked, but not the reply.

"What did he say?"

"He said I was the best friend he had."

12.

The next morning Hannah looked out the window first thing, spotting her wreck of a car, which no magic had transformed overnight. Then she opened the door, looking down toward the road from which no help was on the way. Finally, she hobbled barefoot halfway around the house and looked at the ridge hoping to revive herself, to feel bolstered by the trees that, when winter came, would look implacably different and unbolstering. But now she looked at them with a vague elation. No doubt about it, some of those leaves were turning beautiful again.

It was early October, a month of thirty-one burnished, deep-blue days that were anything but cruel, though usually she found blazing autumn colors so gorgeous, it almost hurt to look. Meadow called them "devil colors" (because of the depths to which red had stooped?), but Hannah reserved judgment hoping, perhaps futilely, to avoid the devil in all his forms. After all, she had successfully avoided God! Or He, her. She had been here nearly a year and on no single day had she bumped headlong into the Maker of Infants. Once when she'd been desperate for a sign, a cricket got under her bed. It sang for hours. That felt very close. It was something she ought to remember on mornings like this one.

Hannah the Wolfe gently
Hannah the Wolfe gently
Hannah the Wolfe gently, it bites
Crunch, crunch, crunch, crunch

"I didn't come here to keep you company," muttered Hannah. He continued chewing like a metronome, ruining everything, so she went back inside to help Meadow get ready for school. Damn it,

Saturday again, Meadow stayed home. That meant she'd have to pull herself together. Crunch, crunch, crunch, crunch: Now it was stuck there!

Sebastian was sitting at the table talking to Meadow who was eating a sandwich, which he had apparently fixed for her. Neither of them looked up when Hannah walked in. Sebastian was overly absorbed in showing Meadow a pocketknife, was demonstrating its sharpness by slicing a long strand of auburn hair, which he dangled in the air.

Morning, sandwiches, and knives, a triad she didn't want to hear. She had no use for unnatural music.

"What kind of breakfast is that supposed to be?"

"Honey and butter, Ma," Meadow answered wearily.

Hannah turned to Sebastian, a deepening line between her eyes. "If you're going to feed her, at least give her a glass of milk."

"Yes, Ma'am," he replied, on the verge of some tone he narrowly missed, so Hannah called down a correction. "Sebastian, would you please stop kicking the table leg? It's very annoying."

"Certainly, Hannah, certainly."

Meadow giggled, and Hannah felt even worse. She wouldn't feel better till Sebastian left.

"Listen, Ian, it may not come as a surprise that I need time to think, so I'd consider it a friendly gesture on your part to head home. This house is too small for much company."

"I have the perfect solution," he said, still making sparkly eyes at her daughter. "Meadow and I will amuse ourselves outside. You can have the whole house to brood in."

"That doesn't suit me."

"Please, Ma? He's gonna play at the pond with me. He already promised. Please? I wanna show him all the bugs. I can catch grasshoppers with my bare fingers now! That brown gunk isn't poison at all! And when you throw 'em in, the fishes gobble 'em up real fast just like this. She popped O's with her mouth to demonstrate. "He's gonna help me feed all the wild fishes. Please?"

Hannah stood looking at her.

"Please?"

"Do it fast," she answered shortly, and went about her business as best she could, which meant she feigned work until they were out of the house, then she flopped down on the couch. She'd never gotten to sleep last night.

I know what I'll do, she thought. I'll write Sebastian the classic Dear John letter and hide it in his pack. He won't read it until he gets home; that will spare me a scene. Oh, the cleverness of Hannah Wolfe!

She rolled over the edge till she could reach the grapefruit box where she kept her various papers. It was a shallow, heavily waxed cardboard box that she lifted off the floor onto her lap like a portable desk. From it she withdrew a yellow legal pad and ballpoint pen with which she began to write.

> Dear Sebastian,
>
> I suspect this note will anger you more and for that, I'm sorry. There is something, though, that must be said.
>
> You and I are not cut out for one another. Not as lovers, not as friends, not even as siblings on the road. I always knew that, but didn't follow my better judgment, which is probably the story of my life.
>
> You're right. I am some sort of hermit. My essential bond is with Meadow, and even that may disappear in a few years when she grows up and leaves me. What God has in store at that point is not clear, but I don't think my path has anything to do with your mental images or even, frankly, with you. I'm sorry to be so blunt, but I want you to understand I am serious. Please do not come to visit me anymore. Good luck, and God bless.
> Hannah

Feeling the need to be decisive, she licked the envelope as quickly as possible. Ian's pack was still where he had left it the night before when she had commented on the fact it looked heavy. She hadn't expected *then* to mail a letter there.

"Open your mouth and close your eyes and you will get a big surprise," she said, pinching one of its hard canvas bulges. "What on earth; you've been swallowing books."

She took out one and looked at it – something Hindu-ish, the title didn't stick. But flipping through its pages, she was startled to see an exotic couple carnally positioned, plainly drawn in the act of intercourse. On each page, this gaudy couple became more experimental. The first pictures were copies of authentic-looking Hindu art, but they soon gave way to everyday originals, variations on a theme now involving the exotic couple and animals.

Biting her lip, Hannah told herself she wasn't jarred. "I'm not easily offended," she told herself. "I've been around too much."

Closing that book, she reached for another, this time pulling out a sketch pad. She opened it, only to gape at a drawing of herself in a crude, stylized pose. Then a sketch of Sebastian, meditating lotus style as she danced before him. For her nipples he had substituted little eyes. Two, swollen, phallic braids fell behind her shoulders, snaking their way through her thighs and toward him. The figures were finely inked, but their objective excellence did nothing to cushion the blow of being used. How dare you do such a slinchy thing, she thought, just as Sebastian and Meadow walked in the door.

"Caught in the act of prying," he said. "Naughty Hannah."

"Meadow, Sebastian and I are going to walk down to the road and back. You wait here."

"Ah, Ma, we just came in for a drink."

"Get your drink, but don't leave this house. Come on, Sebastian, and here – don't forget your *pack*." She threw it at him as savagely as she could under the weighty circumstances.

As they walked out the door, he called over his shoulder, "It's back to the pond in no time."

"Like fun it is," yelled Hannah.

She stomped and he ambled, two disagreeable buffoons headed down her ridiculously uneven slope. Part of her watched, having to admit that for whatever reasons, her life lacked nobility. It was puffed and grand with anger, and nearly broken at times with strange forms of tenderness, but it was not noble, not many things, but especially not noble. How ironic, since she had felt drawn six years ago to a true high-mindedness, and had pledged herself more than ten months ago to the long-renowned summoning power of less being more.

As of this moment, her efforts had brought her here, to this absurd, ugly stretch of dirt where she was soon to deliver through clenched teeth, an absurd, ugly speech. She felt she had no choice, though she *could* try a merely absurd speech first and see if it worked. But the ugliness wanted out.

Sebastian broke in on her thoughts. "Meadow is going to blame me for disappointing her, you know. She looks on me as a friend, and it hardly seems fair -- "

"Well, she looks on *me* as her mother, and if I tell her she can't go to the pond, she accepts it. She certainly won't blame you."

"Because she's Little Miss Good?"

Hannah gave him a scornful look. "Oh, shut up and leave her goodness alone."

"Which reminds me, what were you doing snooping in my pack? Haven't I heard you cast numerous aspersions on that landlord of yours for his faults in that area? For all Justin's imperfections, he would never dream of going through my personal belongings."

Hannah slapped the side of her cheek at the wages of sin. "What if I get reincarnated as a frog?"

"Beware, Hannah. The climb to infinity leaves one groundless."

"If you have something to say, Ian, just spit it out in ordinary words."

Pedantically, he lifted one long finger. "Listen well: You have not grasped the Master's teaching."

She stopped abruptly, overcome. Her life, their conversation, his Master! It was all a cartoon. By their very nature, cartoons aren't noble. What did her revolting, caricatured existence have to do with the real and living God, with the Lord of Heaven and Earth?

"Your Master's teaching squeaks, that's what I think. It's a little toy you made up. All you talk is mish-mash. What are you playing, Buddhist, Hindu, Swahili, or what? What kind of fake religion was that in your pack? Trying to make me into some Near-Eastern, American Indian, gutter saint? Am I another image you've drawn to look at in your closet?" The ugly speech was being given. "Here. Wanna fool with my braid?" She pulled a hank of hair away from her head and offered it to him. "You worship whores, so go ahead."

She finished the last sentence on the ground where he had pushed her. In a split second she had recovered enough to stick up her chin and notice, accidentally, how angry he was. Seething. When he spoke, it was in a shrill, compulsive monotone.

"You've gone too far, Hannah. Last night and now this. I disavow it. Completely. Our relationship." Spit was coming out of his mouth. "Right now. Here. On this spot, I sever all ties with you." He trembled with rage.

The fall had sobered her. "Good, Sebastian, that's entirely the best thing. It was comedy from the beginning. But I did go too far. Let me say – sitting on the ground – that I'm sorry I insulted your religion, whatever it is. I was wrong, and I consider being pushed down a fair trade. But never touch me again. Go home and never come back."

She expected he would do just that, leave as quickly as she hoped. Instead he gave her a look that reminded her of a rabid dog, unhinged and about to run toward her.

"I have one question to ask you. What do you have against me? I refuse to be dismissed like that."

"That's not important at this point. Just go away." She kept her voice low.

"My drawings? Because of my drawings?"

"Your illusions. Because of your illusions."

He looked stunned. "I have no idea what you're talking about. You've shattered the only illusion I've had – that you were more spiritual than the sluts over the ridge."

Hannah shrugged it off.

"What about you?" he sneered.

"What about me? I'm just Hard-hearted Hannah the Vamp of Savannah."

"Yours is the life of illusion. I happen to know."

"Listen, Sebastian, I'm not interested in what you happen to know about me. I thought I was going to have a lot to say to you, but it turns out I don't. Let's just 'sever our tie,' as you put it, and forget the whole thing."

"I have something to say, something most enlightening."

"I don't wanna hear it."

"You shall though. You shall hear the truth about that adorable daughter of yours. You can run, Hannah, but you can't hide from the truth. The one who shatters is shattered."

"Leave Meadow out of it."

He took a deep draught of air, enough to hold him until he was well into his barrage. "She's bad, Hannah, she's Little Miss Bad, do you hear me? She's cruel to animals. She *mutilates* them. She leaves them lying around the pond in pieces. Right now she's sitting up there so obediently with my knife in her pocket, and Hannah," he lowered his voice to a whisper, "ask her what she just used it for."

"I hate your guts, I really do."

"And my art and my body and my religion. But you'll never hate your daughter, will you? Because she's an illusion that you need."

Sure of his timing, he turned and fled back up the slope like a man with something after him. Hannah watched him from the ground until she was sure he'd turned toward the pond and away from her house. Then she mashed her face into a tire track and began to cry the way you can when you're all alone.

13.

"And it happened at pure midnight, when all the hooty owls were flying around outside, eating the mice and the cats. All the cats except you and all the mice except me. You hold still, Big Eyes, I'm just getting to the scary part." Meadow pushed Antlers back into the musical rocking chair that sat in one corner of her room. He was wearing a doll's bonnet hardly large enough to cover one ear. The other ear twitched restively along with his tail, but his efforts to escape remained half-hearted. Every time he edged forward or his storyteller thrust him back, the chair tinkled out another portion of "Mary Had a Little Lamb."

"Meadow, cats don't like to have things tied under their chins. It doesn't feel good." Hannah had been standing in the doorway for several minutes. "They don't like to rock either."

"I'm not rocking him! He's doing it himself." She was sitting on the floor with an eloquent back toward her mother.

"Can't you see he doesn't like it?"

"I'm telling him a real good story."

"Meadow, he doesn't like it, let him go."

The child stood up, pulled off the bonnet easily without untying the strings and backed away from the cat, who made a flaccid getaway.

"Thank you. Now I'd like you to come over here and talk to me a minute." Hannah was glad to see that Meadow's expression, when she turned, was less defiant than her back. The mild reluctance Hannah saw there faded into diffidence as soon as Meadow faced her.

"Your face is all muddy, Ma."

"Am I dirty?" said Hannah, surprised that, as a matter of fact, she could feel the caked-on mud with the tips of her fingers. "You ought to write a song about me and mud-pie cheeks."

Meadow smiled, giving Hannah the opportunity to do the same. She wondered if her daughter would ask to go to the pond, would ask where Ian was, would ask about the mud. But Meadow only smiled shyly. She had a charming mouth that Hannah did not want to be fooled by, even when it was closed.

"Baby, Sebastian went home, but he said he left his knife with you. We'll have to mail it back."

"I don't have it."

"He said you did."

"I think it's at the pond. Yeah, now I remember. Ian *did* leave it at the pond."

"Are you sure?"

"Uh huh. I'm pretty sure."

Hannah mustered her nerve. "How come you two were playing with a knife? Those things are dangerous."

Meadow shrugged; it was a peaked gesture, the kind that knows, but won't tell. It was a shrug that made Hannah's head begin to ache. She pressed her hand hard against her forehead, glad for a moment's cold relief from the sudden throbbing pain.

"I really do want to know what you were doing with the knife."

"Cutting things," said Meadow slowly, her eyes wide.

"What things?"

"Grass."

"Grass?"

"*Some* grass."

Hannah took care to breathe out and in and out, as if this were an ordinary day. "Well, I'll tell you what, Meadow. I'll walk over to the pond and pick up Ian's knife. Is it right there where you usually play?"

"I think so."

"Okay. When I come back, we'll talk some more. Knives aren't meant for children."

The little girl nodded dismally. It was all Hannah could do to turn away. She wanted to run to Meadow for comfort, like a child to her mother. She wanted to hear that the lamb's fleece was white as snow.

The shack had water good enough to wash with, but none of it was hot. If cold wouldn't do, Hannah heated some in a kettle, either on the cook stove or on a small gas burner Simpson had given her for summer use.

It would have been good to wash her face now with a soothing hot cloth (a sure sign of the season's transition), but she was too edgy to stand around the burner and wait. Instead, she went to the sink and splashed her face with the cold water of old rains, rubbing the streaks of dried mud into new life on her cheeks. Washing her face this way wasn't pleasant, only necessary, like walking to the pond.

She talked to herself as she made her way across the field. She ordered the outside world with each step – forming it, informing it – till she had willed an ordinary setting, one which would hold lost pocketknives, but nothing else.

"That's the problem. One, I'm always seeing carnage where there is none. Two, I'm always scared. Three, there's gotta be something wrong with the way I see. Four, I see too much. Five, what isn't even there."

When it came right down to it, wasn't everything simple? It was only a matter of breaking reality down, chopping it into bite-size sentences so you wouldn't choke on the whole thing at once.

She walked as fast as possible, her eyes avoiding the ground she hurried over. She certainly didn't want to inspect it, had no desire at all to look down when those magnificent trees along the ridge were almost ready to burn with color. It was a day for taking things in sweeps like tourists do. After she found the knife, she'd stand back to make one last panoramic search of the area. She must also practice a clement speech of caution to give to Meadow.

Making a careful turn, Hannah prepared her mind for something odd and ridiculous: — black banana, yes surely that. Someone had dropped a half-eaten banana, and it had gone black in the sun. Raw bananas always go black in the sun, even in the house.

The object she turned back to see *was* half-eaten. The sun had sucked out his eyes, but something else had chewed his legs off. He was only the short, black stub of a frog by now, dried enough to look like an ancient mummy and equally royal. Though his eyes were mere sockets, his head held true at a stiff proud angle that gave him the look of a creature who stubbornly denied his own catastrophe, one who hadn't broken down at the ruin of himself.

It was difficult for Hannah to believe what she saw, no matter how far she leaned down to look. She peered at the hard, wrinkled stub and told it that Antlers hadn't meant to be so cruel. He didn't know how long it took for the sun to bake a crippled frog to death. "You've obviously gotten old here," she said. "Dead first, then old."

With the edge of her flip flop, she tipped him over and rolled him out of the way into some weeds where he could crumble to the blackest of powder in tactful seclusion. She straightened herself. "I don't want to think about it," she announced, fixing her gaze at the ridge in all its latent splendor, and in perfect oblivion made it a dozen steps more to where Meadow usually played.

The knife was exactly where her daughter said it would be. That liar, Sebastian! But even before she bent down, she saw the others close by. There were three frogs; shriveled, black vessels emerging one by one; unwelcome visitors. No, it was she who had come to them, and they welcomed her inscrutably, more like closed doors than opened.

Then the ache. She found herself staring at a creature whose sockets still had eyes. He was quite alive, looking in her direction with cool indifference, taking no notice of his legs, which lay severed beside him.

Hannah trembled, moving closer in spite of her aversion, so close she was kneeling beside the frog who rested on his membraned belly, unnaturally tranquil. Repulsed, she took a closer look, noticing the softest movement in his throat. Its flutter made her think of eyelids, and she almost gagged.

And where were his legs? She could only count three on the ground. The last one could be anywhere, even under her hand or knee. She jumped back at the thought, afraid she would find the fourth one stuck to her, making its grotesque escape the only way it could.

Choking on tears she was too angry to shed, Hannah marched her daughter back to the pond. Meadow had spent ten long minutes delaying in the outhouse, a ruse her mother had allowed for one selfish reason, she needed time herself.

Her hands were shaking so much, she gave up trying to open a new bottle of aspirin, throwing it against the wall as a second choice before she stalked outside to find a switch. But it had been the wrong time of year for that ritual; whatever she found was dry, fit only for kindling. The few moments of preparation she'd given herself had yielded nothing except deep disgust at her practical ineptitude.

"*What*? *What* were you doing? *What*, Meadow, *what* were you possibly doing?"

The little girl only whimpered.

"What?" came the question again.

"Playing like a cat."

"For God's sake! No, you weren't! You wanna know who you were playing like? Like that horse killer. Like that horrible stupid horse killer!"

Meadow shook her head, refusing to accept her mother's comparison. "First, I was playing cat. I *was*. Then Ian said I was playing school. School's okay to play. He said so."

Hannah stopped walking. "Who plays school by killing things? Oh, I get it. Ian and you were just doing a biology experiment, right?" Meadow nodded, and Hannah continued the march. "Don't gimme that. You don't even know what a biology experiment is. You're just making excuses for yourself, little girl, and I'm not buying *any* of them. Hear me?" She stopped again. "Why don't you just tell the truth and admit you wanted to do it for the fun of it? You were thinking all about Meadow and not one tiny bit about the frog. That's right, isn't it?"

Meadow wiped her eyes with her arm and whispered "Yes."

"Well, good for you," said Hannah. "We're getting somewhere. Now look here. Who did that?" She pointed to the mummified stub in the weeds.

"I can't see it."

"Right down there. Did you do that?"

"No."

"How many did you do?"

"Only one, I promise. Antlers did the rest. I just carried them all in one place to make a graveyard."

"You're sure that's all you hurt? One?"

"And some grasshoppers."

"How'd you hurt the grasshoppers?"

Meadow started to cry and didn't answer.

"*How*, Meadow?"

"Different ways."

"Okay, come on. It's been awhile since you've seen this fellow. You've been inside getting a drink and telling stories to your cat. This frog – here he is – this little playmate of yours has been sitting in the sun wondering where his legs went. Maybe frogs need a drink too. How's he gonna get one?" She looked in her daughter's face and was grateful to see shame.

"He can't, I guess."

"He sure can't. You guess 100 percent right."

Meadow squatted down and stared at the frog, then she got back up to hunt for something. When the child came back, she had a large, yellow leaf in her hand, which she used to pick up the wasted creature.

"Now what?"

"I'm putting him back in the pond where he lives."

"That frog's not gonna swim, Meadow, he's gonna drown. Because frogs swim with their legs. And he doesn't have any legs. I can't think of a thing you can do to help him. His pond is like a coffin now."

The look of pain on her daughter's face slowed Hannah down. "Well, go ahead. Dunk him in the water and set him down in the weeds somewhere. Maybe he can catch a bug if you cool him off first."

"I'm sorry, Frog," Meadow whispered, tears sliding down her cheeks. "I'm sorry I played with you like that. Please don't die." She turned to her mother. "Is he gonna die, Ma? I didn't do anything to his middle body."

"It doesn't matter, Meadow. What you did is going to kill him."

The little girl swished him around once more, still weeping. "Do you know I'm sorry, frog?" she asked. "Does he, Ma?"

Hannah felt a lump in her throat, a sign her anger was waning. "Maybe he does, I don't know. I believe that God knows you're sorry."

"I hope God tells him."

"Come on, Meadow, let's go on home."

"Are you gonna spank me?"

"Do you think you need it?"

"I dunno."

"I don't know either."

A full moon, the last straw. Never had she spent such a disturbing twenty-four hours, and now when she needed some small form of oblivion like sleep, in poured the moon with all its whacking influences. Insomnia, a joke to wrap things up in style. Lunar Insomnia and the Little Mad House; that had possibilities. Maybe the Cowboy needed a band to back him up.

Outside, from the tree beyond her open window, came the insistent call of a whippoorwill. Loud and right outside her window: whippoorwill, whippoorwill, whippoorwill.

"Stop it, Bird," she begged. "I need sleep or I'll never make it, I'll cave in completely."

Whip her well, whip her well, whip her well.

She might have known he'd have something to say. "I would never whip her well enough for *you*, would I? You'd like me to whip her all day long."

The strumming stopped, but she could sense his hand poised, ready to accompany his sinister words, his sick lyrics. In the silvery light she heard his breathing, so real that everything told her she was doomed. In the middle of an October night, in her own bed while ferociously clutching a pillow and straining to hear, she acknowledged her own doom and the uselessness of struggle.

"You are not part of this blackness," she told the Cowboy, praying past him into the depths where God was Being Himself in the dark. "You may be the despicable occasion of it, but even now I can utterly renounce all your songs and comments and your stupid guitar, which isn't worth spit. I smash your guitar over your evil-humored head and utterly renounce you."

Se-bastard White won my fight,
And now Miss Ass-ter's courtin' disaster

"Go ahead, sing me another one," she mumbled victoriously.

Breath, the sound of breath, made her hold her own. She wasn't scared, but held her own breath to listen to that of someone else. It sounded old and leaky around the edges. "Come on in, Mr. Simpson. I know you're out there."

14.

It was a wild guess, but she knew she was right. What she didn't know was what would happen next, whether she could expect him to vanish without a trace, or whether that was his plan for her. Finally grounded in general doom, she was hardly even curious. In any case, it rapidly became clear that neither of them was disappearing.

"Hey, peeping ears, come inside and I'll drink a cup of coffee with you. I've got insomnia and it's keeping me awake. Might as well have a cup of coffee."

He wasn't jumping at the offer. These peeping Toms were suspicious, like wild woodland creatures, perpetually nervous. What more should she say?

"I've never known anyone who did what you're doing, but I haven't forgotten you warned me, and I sympathize with your awkward predicament. Don't be scared, I won't hit you with the baseball bat."

She heard him move. He was changing positions before he spoke in a voice that sounded surprisingly ordinary. "I made a solemn promise to God Almighty, I'd never step foot inside this house of mine so long as you lived here, Hannah. It was my way of looking out for you." There was still no face at the window.

"J. Norris, I'm *inviting* you in. A night like this, we can't stand on ceremony."

"I'm not coming," he said presently. "I made a promise I knew I could keep, and I'm keeping it."

"Didn't figure you could promise not to look in my window, huh?" He made no comment. "Never mind, J. Norris, I'll make coffee and come out there."

Before bed, she'd hauled her flannel nightgown out of the trunk. It was a roomy, colorless garment rough with matted fuzz balls, and long before she'd hauled it out of the trunk, she'd hauled it out of her mother's giveaway box. "Won't catch a man with that," Lucille had teased.

"Perfect outfit for a tryst with Simpson," chuckled Hannah. But just in case, she wore blue jeans under it, and wrapped a shawl around her shoulders. "Don't go away! The water has to boil. It won't take long; I'll use the bottled gas."

This was going to be interesting. How unfortunate it was one of those occasions that her mother wouldn't want to know about, and that Meadow wouldn't understand. With Sebastian out of the picture, there was no one to pass it on to. Maybe that's what being a hermit meant – just her and her companion Night, who was also taking it in first hand. Simpson fished in the same lonely waters. She didn't figure his wife would want to hear about it either.

"Well, I hardly know where to begin," she said, handing him a mug of steaming coffee.

"Thank you, Hannah." He was still standing by the tree, right under his sign, she noticed.

"Do you know where to begin? I mean, surely this situation calls for an appropriate response."

"If you was my wife, I'd call the Sheriff."

"You'd get in a lot of trouble."

"Mebbe trouble's what I need. I've had this notion that the Lord was giving me time, waiting on me like a merciful judge till I could solve this thing myself. But I never could. I knowed it was wrong, and I knowed I'd have to be punished when my time ran out. I don't blame nobody but myself."

"You blamed me some for tempting you."

"That was yesterday," he replied, matter-of-fact.

Hannah sighed. "I'm guilty, don't worry."

"Humph."

The sound didn't tell her whether he agreed or not. She wasn't even sure *she* agreed, but she put it forth as a safe assumption. "J.

Norris, I don't know about you, but I feel sort of wobbly. I gotta sit down."

"You want rheumatism before your time? Setting on damp ground, that's what you'll get."

He crouched down beside her and she wondered how a man his age could be so limber. A long time ago he must have been wiry.

"Bet you used to climb this tree."

"Every day and then some. Don't have the breath now."

"That's how I knew you were out here. You kept hidden, but I heard you breathing."

There wasn't much to say, so they sat together in the dim gray light and resolutely stared at nothing except the sootiness that enveloped his barn further down the hill. She was stricken by the sight. There weren't numbers enough to count how many things lay safely concealed in the cache of night. Even during the day, some great effort was made to keep things safe by camouflage. But she was out in the open, an orphan forgotten in the light

"Have you watched me ever since I've been here?"

"Hannah, it's mighty hard to explain myself."

"I'm not asking you to explain, I just wanna know what's been happening. I mean, every night when I went to bed, were you waiting outside my window?"

"It ain't that bad."

"I'm trying to remember all the things you said. Like when you got so upset about my hippie boyfriend."

"It's one thing to see a woman alone. It's something else to see her with a man."

The realization of all Simpson had seen washed over Hannah and almost made her angry at him. "Last night, were you here then?"

He nodded his head.

"And you saw everything? You saw Ian and me?"

He nodded again.

She poured the rest of her coffee on the ground as she began to cry in long gulps, just between herself and God.

"I'd comfort you, but I reckon you don't want to be touched."

"I don't. Thanks anyway."

"Here's a clean rag for your nose."

She snatched it out of his hand and rubbed it hard against her eyes. "I'm so stupid. My life is so stupid, so *crammed full* of stupidity. There's not anything that makes sense."

"If it's any comfort, half the time I believe I belong in the loony bin."

Hannah blew her nose. "You might belong in the loony bin, but I belong in Loony Tunes."

"Don't go turning on yourself. You're a good woman. I seen it the day I rented you this place. I even said to myself, 'Poor as she is, she's too good for me'."

"Mr. Simpson, what if I *had* liked you better? What if I did want you as a special friend?"

He looked further off in the distance. "The Lord spared us some misery, I reckon. We're best off never to know. There's one thing I do know, Hannah, which is how I prayed I'd only want to look. And until that skinny fellow in them Roman sandals started visiting, that's how it was. You and Meadow looked good as gold, like you was pictures in some book that was old and heavy as the Bible. But life is better because the stories in it are all mixed together. You weren't on no page, you was right inside a house that belongs to me. My own mother took to housekeeping in those four walls. And take that table in there, my grandpa made it. Hell, you're living with a real antique! The longer you was here, the more it seemed like we was linked in some unearthly fashion, and I'd commence to thinking you felt the same. But that beau of yours brought everything back down to here and now. When he come on the scene, I knew you'd soon look different."

"Like a slut, that's how you made me feel, long before Ian came around. I always thought you poked your nose in like a whorehouse janitor who took pleasure in cleaning up."

Her words made him start. "The two of us walk a thin line between God-fearing and trash. It might not show, but I been trying to keep us both on the upwind side of ourselves."

"I gotta whiff, though." She sighed and turned in his direction.

"It won't kill you, I reckon, otherwise I wouldn't be here to tell of it."

"Probably not," she agreed, feeling the night slip out from under her like a tide. If only it would kindly wash her out to sea. "Nothing seems to kill me. I always wake up to each new day, stranded here in Kentucky as usual. Which reminds me. I've decided to go back to Cincinnati. Either place I'm stranded, but up there it's easier to wait. Maybe God will make Himself more present farther north."

"You say you're fixing to leave?"

"Yep. Gonna head back to Cincinnati."

"Listen girl, your car don't run."

"I know it. I was wondering if you'd loan me money to get something else? You can keep my Chevy. I mean, all four tires are new, and maybe you could even use the rest of it. I'm not trying to blackmail you or anything. I'd pay you back."

"Lord a-mighty, I owe you that much. I'd welcome the chance to give you a car if you wouldn't refuse."

"I might refuse a fancy green pickup. Get me something with a little less power."

"How soon would you be needing one?"

"No hurry. Well, as soon as I can. Before the first freeze at least. In a few days? I sure appreciate your offer."

"Think nothing of it." He stood up and handed her his empty cup. "You and Meadow still looks as good as gold. I'll be saying good night now, though."

"Won't your wife wonder where you've been?"

"She knows I walk of a night."

"Oh, yeah, good night, J. Norris." She held out her hand and he shook it. "I'll wash your handkerchief for you."

"No need."

"I wouldn't dream of giving it back dirty." She raised her night-gown and stuffed it into the pocket of her jeans. "Besides, I might cry some more."

When she got inside, she had to laugh at how startled he was when she raised her gown. But after that she thought about other things that made her cry. "I did die at night," she wept, "and it *was* slapstick all the way. I hope you don't want an encore, I'm way too tired." Letting herself be carried, she closed her eyes and was swiftly borne into a good night's sleep.

15.

Meadow woke with the sun in her window and played quietly till she couldn't see it, however far beyond the sill she leaned. It was evident her mother was especially tired because she didn't stir when Meadow whispered questions. Even if she whispered them directly into Hannah's ear, there was no response, so the child amused herself, still subdued from the day before. Actually, Hannah heard her humming, but only as part as a mellow dream in which an older man named Henry Ford was patting her tenderly on the back. "Are you still single?" he whispered, and with great reluctance she told him no, she had committed herself to another.

When she did wake, it was to the sound of a clapping chant. "Sunday! Sunday! Sunday is the Sun's day! Monday! Monday! Monday is the Mon's day!"

"Monday is the Moon's day," mumbled Hannah. She pushed herself up on her knees, shaggy and flustered. "What's today, Sunday or Monday?"

"No school today," sang Meadow.

"Vunder bar," intoned her mother, swaying like a wounded beast.

"Hey, Ma, get up. I'm starved as a skeleton."

"I don't blame you a bit, Babe. Don't worry about it." She settled back down on her stomach.

"Ma! I want something to eat!"

"Fix yourself a honey and butter sandwich."

"I tried, but the honey lid's stuck on."

"Okay, hang on. Gimme another minute." The truth was she felt pretty good, downright happy even, though it was news to some of her muscles.

"Hey, Meadow Mouse, I've got a surprise."

The child lost no time jumping under the covers with her. “Tell me!” she said, and then as an afterthought, “You aren’t mad at me this day are you?”

“No, I’m not mad at you this day. This is a day to forgive everyone. I forgive you and you forgive me.”

“What for?”

“You tell me.”

“I forgive you for making me take off Antler’s bonnet when it wasn’t even hurting him.”

“Thank you, Mouse.”

“Now tell me the surprise!”

“We’re moving back to Cincinnati. Very soon.”

“Oh boy, I can see Judy! I’ve been missing her ever since we left.”

“Really? You never said that before.”

“I didn’t want you to feel bad.”

Hannah pulled her daughter closer, into the chair she made by pulling up her knees. “You’re a good girl, Meadow. I love you, you know that? I love you, I love you.”

“Me too,” said Meadow. “I love you back.”

“Oh no you don’t,” teased Hannah. “You love me front, it’s the wall that’s loving me back.”

“I don’t get it.”

“That’s ’cause it’s not too gettable. I’m a little woozy this morning, you’ll have to forgive me.”

“Because this is the day, huh? All day we’ve got to forgive each other.”

“Right.”

“I’ll forgive you *if* you’ll sing me a song!”

“Oh no, I couldn’t possibly think up a song this morning.”

“Please Ma? I know you can. You always can if you want to.”

“Is that so? I just grind them out?”

“Yep.”

Meadow handed her an oblong piece of air. “Thanks, Sugar,” said Hannah. “We want folks to hear us.” She closed her eyes to let it all come, then spoke into the object she pretended to hold. "I'd like to dedicate this ballad to all the stranded fish in the sea." She began on a soft, plaintive note ...

> Oh your kind knowing's goin' — before us,
> in every place that you dwell,
> And your kind knowing's goin' — before us,
> as far as I can tell,
> Oh your kind knowing's goin' — before us,
> to the cliffs of Tuscany,
> And it's awful long, oh it's awful strong,
> It's called your sub-lim-ity."

"There, that's the very best my subconscious can manufacture without a cup of coffee."

"Your songs are so good," said Meadow wistfully. "I wish I could write songs like that."

"I thought it was gonna be about Cincinnati," answered Hannah, returning the microphone to her daughter, who took it. "Are you gonna like moving back to the city? There's gonna be lots of people and not so many wild animals."

Pain crossed Meadow's face and Hannah held her even closer, abashed at raising old ghosts. From now on she intended to look ahead, to leave shadows to the shadows.

Hannah wasn't surprised when later that afternoon they heard the roar of Simpson's truck as it barreled up the slope. To hear and not despise increased her happiness.

"Fear is the Devil's something and Hate is his something else," she announced, groping for an aphorism. "Just think, J. Norris Simpson is driving up to the house, and I feel no rancor." She listened to the grind of his downshift. "A little cacophony," she muttered, "nothing serious." She met him at the door with a genuine welcome.

"Well, good morning J. Norris."

"Afternoon, Hannah. You sound mighty pert."

"Got bells on my toes. What'cha got there?"

"Brung you the Sunday paper. Thought now you're going out in the world, it might help you to know what's happening."

"Who's killing who, huh?" She did sound cheerful.

"And this here's the funny papers for Meadow." Looking past Hannah, he craned his neck to see her. "The way I've seen you sit glued to all them cartoons down at my place, I reckon you'll like these too."

He looked back at her mother. "Now, when you get back to the city, I hope you buy that child a T.V. set. It don't make no sense to live in the Middle Ages."

"Baloney," chided Hannah, careful to smile.

"It's not just me that thinks it, Ma does too. You got to learn to listen to good advice, Hannah. Being clever and different from other folks don't assure you of a solid life."

"I fully agree."

"I'm glad to hear it," he said, finally handing her the newspaper. By the way he stood there, she felt obligated to invite him in, though she knew perfectly well that wasn't his mute request.

"No, I don't believe I will, thank you. You're still living here, Hannah. I wouldn't have no self-respect left if I did."

"That's fine, don't explain. It seems to me, though, you have something else you wanna say. Have you changed your mind about the car?"

He looked hurt. "I have not," he declared. "Once I give my word, in a matter, it's settled. What kind of man are you used to?"

Hannah produced a smirk at her own expense. "Well, let's not get into *that*."

"You must of read my mind. I ain't done. I come up here to tell you about a certain situation that's developed."

"Don't go bringing me any bad news, now!"

"I wish I could avoid it, I surely do."

"It *is* bad news? I hope it's not my mother..."

"No, no nothing like that. It's about that youngster who's been bothering you. It's a long story, Hannah, so in case I forget, I said

I'd come up here and retrieve his pocketknife, which it's not surprising to hear, he stole."

"Oh my gosh, what happened?"

"Now hold on. This is a long story and it'll take me some time to lay it out right. If you'd just fetch me the knife before I forget all about it?"

"We don't have it. I think I left it on the ground at the pond. Please hurry, I hate suspense."

"Well, I didn't waste no time driving up here to tell you this, so don't pitch a fit. There's this man, see, he knocked on my door about noon, I'd say, and asked me to help straighten things out. Halfways, he was wanting you, but he couldn't find his way up here, I reckon, without a paved road. A city feller. But I will say in his behalf, he was a fine respecter of private property and perhaps that's why he come to me first. It's his father's knife, by the way, and it means a lot to him.

"J. Norris! I'm waiting to hear what happened!"

"I'm aiming to tell you, girl! Keep your britches on." He reddened at his choice of words, and slowed to a halt.

"*Did* anything happen? You gotta tell me!

"It sure did," he said, relieved to go on. "Young Mister Bald, this is secondhand of course, he nearly lost all the sense God gave him. Started running and hollering about plots against his life and said this woman who lives over the ridge, which means you, was trying to poison him. To hear this feller tell it, the boy nearly hung hisself, but they all held him down so he couldn't do it. The man that come to see me, he looked like some program on the T.V. set, one of those flashy types. Like a detective. *Just* like a detective with this pretty girl hanging on to his hand like she was scared she'd lose her way or something. She didn't say nothing the whole time. Anywho, this feller had a peculiar name, too, something like 'Justice', only I didn't catch it. To tell you the truth, I didn't try all that hard because the way he looked, I lost my concentration. "

"Wait, wait! Is that it? All you know is they stopped him?"

"They didn't let him do it. It took all of them, skinny as he is, but they wrapped him tight up in a blanket so he couldn't do no harm. Later today they might be driving him to some hospital or other, Lexington or Louisville, I can't remember where the feller told me. He was chiefly wanting to ask me what I knew about, you know …"

"This is terrible! I think I should go check on him. Listen, can you drive me over there right now?"

"Hannah, the man was very clear on that point. I won't quote you what he said, but all they want from you is not to disturb things. Hannah, the youngster's *sick*, he thinks you're out to feed him poison. You don't want to get mixed up with troubles like that."

"Does Justin blame *me* for what's happened? He doesn't think it's my fault, does he?"

Simpson labored under this difficulty. "Justin! That's his name. Sounds a bit like 'Justice' don't it?"

"It's perfectly obvious you're not answering my question. What did Justin say about me?"

"Now, you know it's no good to pass things on secondhand. They'll always come out wrong every time. I'll just put it this way, the man was upset and tired hisself being up all night, so he was likely looking to blame another. It seemed to him, though, that anyone could tell the boy wasn't of sound mind. He come to them right from the hospital in the first place. I guess he needed some kind of re-ha-bilitation. They weren't too glad when he started getting it at your place."

"How was I supposed to know? Nobody told me."

"That's the very thing I pointed out, Hannah, but he said you had your own eyes and ears and that you have to give folks credit for some, well, brains is what I think he said, but I told him you didn't lack those. Don't take offense; he was real tired and worried. Fiery, though. Maybe he was more like a preacher from California than a detective. But the way he dressed, Hannah, now that was something else, different from what I've ever seen before. Something about a fully grown man looking like a rainbow that turns my stomach, quite frankly it does. It made him look like a pure circus."

"Who cares if I'm welcome or not!"

Simpson looked at her with pity. "He was real strong on that point, Honey. Said you're to stay out of it, and if you want to help the situation, he said you can always pray."

It seemed to Hannah she'd been standing there so long she was locked in place. Clumsily breaking loose, she turned around to see how Meadow was faring. She'd been so quiet, Hannah had forgotten about her.

"You hear what J. Norris is saying?"

The little girl nodded her head, but didn't look up from the funnies she kneeled upon. "We made Ian get sick."

"*You* didn't, Baby. It was only me."

"I'm already praying," said Meadow. "I know you didn't mean to."

Simpson interrupted apologetically. "Don't trouble yourself searching for that knife. Tomorrow or the next day, I'll be checking the pond myself. Them cattails is spreading like wildfire, and I'm thinking to put in some Aquazene. It kills just about everything, but it don't hurt the cows."

"I can find it," said Hannah, staring at him in disbelief. "Don't poison the water."

16.

Hannah lay on the couch, legs raised and resting on its sausage-like arm. She had been feet first to the wall a good hour, scarcely moving, but alert, watching a corner of the room while Meadow played on the floor and hummed. Gone the flossy tones of earlier. Meadow's hum had lost its careless lilt. Now it was a staid, tuneless, refrigerator sort of sound, one that gave no warning when it faded out the door.

"Hey, Meadow, where do you think you're going?" It wasn't like her to leave the house without a word.

"Huh?"

"I didn't say you could take off somewhere."

"To give my frog a swish."

"Oh, Mouse, he'll be dead by now. Something probably ate him last night."

"Maybe not. I think he could eat a bug if I hold it up to his mouth." She extended her palm to show Hannah several dead flies.

"Don't get your hopes up."

"I know," she said. "Can I go now?"

"Bring home the knife while you're at it."

"Okay, bye Ma."

"Meadow? Be really careful, huh? Wash your hands in the pond because flies are icky, and don't fall in."

"Then you'd *really* stare at nothing."

"That's the truth."

Hannah turned her attention back to the nothing Meadow referred to, an upper corner where, it so happened, she had been watching a spider, the only other source of visible life in the room. "I wonder why Ian thought I was trying to poison him? Is that a reflection on my cooking?" In comparison to her question, the act of addressing the creature directly seemed reasonable. In fact, the spider's serious and busy motion gave her a measure of satisfaction that the wider universe was impervious to her quips and gibes. After consulting her oracle, Hannah attended to its steady designs until the insouciant answer came to her: *It was your poisonous venom.*

Pained by assent, she swung away from so much living matter to another corner where there was only the starkness of long since joined wood. But if you looked at that corner long enough, it too released a message, one she almost resented. What business did it have, fitting together like that for so long? People were loose and unattached. They rolled around like loose marbles in an assortment of containers – shacks, pickups, hospitals. Crazy, a shifting crazy world. It was like a horrible fun house: Once you lost your balance and fell in the rolling cylinder, you couldn't get up again, not unless someone rescued you. Who would rescue Sebastian?

Having framed a sensible question, she felt abysmal doubt until other words followed her across the room: *Imagination cannot help but fail you.* The message lodged in the darkness of her mind, cleansing it somewhat, affording neither more nor less wisdom. Full of trepidation, she pushed aside her doubts, and prayed to her Maker more bravely for help.

At her daughter's return, Hannah felt considerable relief, but it only took one glance to see that the child's mission of mercy had been a useless, even morbid, ordeal.

"How'd it go?"

"He's alive."

"By golly. I'm amazed."

"Only if you poke him. I swished him, but he didn't like it."

"You cooled him off though."

"Yeah, and when I poked him, I was careful that it didn't hurt. But he wouldn't open his mouth for any flies."

"Mouse, switch on the light, will you? It's getting too dark in here."

Meadow flipped on the goose-neck study light Hannah had used in high school. The shack had one electrical socket, so they often had to move the lamp, fully exposing the extension cord. Usually the lamp stayed on a stool, unless they needed to use the stool in another way. The haplessness of this arrangement, Hannah thought, was a fitting comment on their time in Kentucky. No sooner had she made this observation, than the sudden flick of light propelled her to the door.

"Excuse me, Missy, I gotta go outside."

"Hey Ma, what for?"

"I'll be *right* back."

"Are you gonna poop?"

"Gimme five minutes."

It wasn't the outhouse, it was a flash of inspiration. Hannah rounded the corner, patting the tree like an old friend. She'd known someone once who'd gotten arrested looking into his own window at night. He'd had some trouble explaining to the police that he wanted to see what it looked like inside.

At her own window, Hannah was undisturbed. She stood there as long as she could, till Meadow grew restless and wandered to the door in search of her. "My coin," murmured Hannah, humbled by her view of that well-knit healthy body moving within the room to a rhythm all its own. "My pledge." Content with the moment and its wellspring of ancient thought, she backed away in time to meet Meadow who, even half out the door, was sustainingly illumined.

"Boy, it sure does take you a long time. I can go a lot faster than that."

"Meadow, let's you and me go for a walk."

"I'm hungry! We keep forgetting to eat today."

"Good thinking," said Hannah, who wouldn't have otherwise remembered food. "How about a, um, a sandwich?"

"I'm sick of sandwiches."

"I know you are, Mouse, but if you'd eat one more of them, I'd be a grateful lady. My stomach doesn't feel up to fixing much."

"Okay, yellow cheese."

"Please," coached her mother.

"Please," echoed the child.

Opening the refrigerator, Hannah remembered Sebastian and the night there was no beer. Even if she had a six-pack now, she wouldn't drink it. This was not going to be a tipsy walk. She was eager to leave. Maybe Meadow could eat her sandwich outside. "Could you?"

"Could I what?"

"Eat this outside while we're walking? I'll leave it in one piece."

"I will *if* you'll hold my hand. Not my sandwich hand, of course."

"Thanks Meadow. When we get to Cincinnati, I promise to cook more. Lots of scalloped potatoes."

"And casserole?"

"Heaps of casserole. Ready? Want a cup of milk before we go?"

"Nope. How come we gotta hurry?"

"I don't know. There's just this thing I want to do."

"What?"

"You'll see."

A harvest moon was rising in the east, looking different than it had last night when she sat outside with Simpson. "Twice as big and a different color," said Hannah. "You'd never know it's the same silver moon we're use to."

"Is it?" said Meadow between bites.

"Sure. The moon just changes its look a lot. More than the sun."

"How come?"

"To make life more interesting."

She'd become proficient walking at night so they headed down the slope without a flashlight. It wasn't necessary to have one when the moon was full, but even on those nights too dark to see a hand, she could do without. She guided herself by the feel of the ground and the sounds her feet made. Spongy soil, weeds, ruts; she'd learned they all felt different. It didn't take a flashlight to keep you on course, only attention and memory.

Since most of the trees were gone, so was the crackling of leaves underfoot. But Hannah knew how loud the woods were this time of year. She would like to be told how forest Indians, perhaps relatives of hers, had ever managed stealth in the fall. Or how they had moved at night through virgin timber. That was one good thing, probably the only good thing, about this eroded slope. The stumps, not tall enough to be friends, were too short to be enemies.

Once on the road, they turned right. Now easier walking freed their attention, the better to hear dozens of night sounds that flowed from sources not human. The country was only said to be quiet because the sounds of birds and insects didn't count.

Far off in the distance, a dog barked, sad as any coyote. A lot of them had barked at her when she drove through these knobs the first time. Oh the wonders she had expected, last year.

Meadow, who had quickly finished her sandwich, clung to her mother's hand. She didn't seem interested in where they were going. Hannah took this to mean she felt nervous on the road at night. Her small hand felt like a baby bird, all fragile bone. Was there any duty more poignant than motherhood? If there was, she didn't want to hear of it. This happiness was keen enough, full enough of confounded expectation and the need to be good.

"I've got a riddle for you," Hannah said. "What keeps the moon from falling?"

"I dunno," answered Meadow. "A string?"

"Nope. I think it must be the beams. The moonbeams."

"That's a good one."

"I thought so too."

"I know one! I got it in some bubblegum. What happens if you tell secrets in a cornfield?"

"I'll bet it has something to do with ears."

"Right! If you stand in corn, the corn's ears hear the secrets!"

Hannah held fast to her hand, keeping a brisk pace until they could see the blue glare of Simpson's security light. It splashed an artificial moonlight around his house, claiming everything made visible with a brightness so contrary to the night's true light that for the first time Hannah felt they had been walking in the dark.

As they approached the building, she decided to walk past it, to come in from the other side where there were still some shadows for cover. She hoped for a window through which she could catch a glimpse of Simpson. Not that she planned to look long, just hard.

"Ma, you went past the door!"

"Shh. We're not going inside. I wanna stand in the yard awhile and peek."

"Are we spies?"

"Yep. So be real quiet. We're spying on J. Norris."

"How come?"

"To get a look at the real one."

"The real J. Norris? Are there two?"

"Shh. Yes, but one of them I invented. Shh, there he is."

He walked past them through a dusky hallway on his way to the kitchen.

"Watching T.V. made him hungry," whispered Hannah. They moved deeper down the yard, toward the kitchen light, which had just come on. This time he was clearly visible, though they faced his back. He was cutting himself a piece of something, and talking into another room. When he turned to fill a glass with milk, they saw a cake.

Hannah strained her eyes to see him, wondering if the punishment for this transgression was a squint. No way around it, so she concentrated on her task, entranced. She'd seen Meadow freshly, but sought Simpson new.

"What does he look like?"

"I can't tell yet."

She tried to see what she hadn't seen before. There was the roll of his neck hanging over his khaki work collar, and his flat, broad buttocks, but that was only new because she saw him from a different angle. She was after a glimpse of his weightiness all right, but not of his flesh. She'd come here to be reminded of the weight of *him*, the being within the body within the clothes.

"Almost," she thought. "You're almost a separate work of God."

At that moment Simpson moved to the sink for a dishrag, then back to wipe off the table, and in the lingering of his hand, he turned into a man that Hannah didn't know. Disguised from her, he was nevertheless undisguisedly himself, not a chimera. In less time than it took to be grateful, the seen and unseen merged and focused.

"Well, praise the Lord," thought Hannah. "You were walking the Earth and eating cake that someone else fixed you before I was even born."

"There he goes, Ma."

"For me he just got here."

"That sounds goofy."

"It's too bad we can't go spy on Sebastian."

"Spying's bad isn't it?"

"Your grandmother wouldn't approve and she knows a lot about those things, but I'm hoping God will understand this one time."

"He'll forgive us. Today's the day."

Three more days elapsed before they were in the car and gone, as gone as the real Simpson whom they'd seen leaving the kitchen with his dessert; as gone as Sebastian whom she'd almost known and Justin whom she hadn't; as gone as the horse that got shot and the leaves that were falling, but not on her slope. Gone as the Cowboy. She hoped that was permanent, but she had no way of knowing.

She'd driven down poor and was driving home poorer, back to Cincinnati from which she was now gone. Oh, and her Old Blue Chevy was gone too, but here she was, driving an even older Dodge. Simpson had bought her a good-looking, blue one.

"So many things are gone," said Meadow, "I'm glad Antlers *isn't*."

"Me too," said her mother.

"Who's the Cowboy?"

"Some guy that used to provoke me like that booger Kenny, only the Cowboy is a bigger booger and lives in my attic," said Hannah, tapping her head. "It's sort of a joke. Nothing I can explain."

"Kenny's gone!" bubbled Meadow.

"Cupcake Day is gone," seconded Hannah, "but Friday isn't."

"Grandma's gone, but she's been gone ever since we moved here."

"That's true," said Hannah. "Let's visit her soon. I'm lonesome."

"Me too. She *loves* cats. And I know something else that's very gone."

"What's that?"

"The knife ... yucky." She wiped the yuckiness off her fingers onto her pants.

"We never did find that, did we?"

There was a noticeable gap in the conversation, one that lasted till Hannah realized her question had precipitated a crisis. It was a panicked waif who sat beside her.

"My gosh, Meadow, what's the matter? Don't look so insecure."

"I can't help it. I'm scared of you right now."

"There certainly has been a change in the weather. Does it have something to do with the knife?"

"I found it, but I didn't tell you."

"Why not?"

"You wanted me to bring it home."

"Why didn't you?"

"Because I threw it in the pond."

That wasn't surprising. She herself had thrown her father's belt away. After he'd used it to spank her for plucking off the heads of all the neighbor's dahlias, she'd hated the sight of it. "Because that knife reminded you of unpleasant things?"

"No, because Ian threw it at me."

There was a shift in the chemistry of Hannah's body. Blood thinned to water in her head, shoulders, and arms, while in her legs it thickened like curds in whey. With effort, she slogged one foot onto the brake and pulled off the road.

"When did this happen? Don't look so scared, I'm not mad at you."

"Oh, you know," Meadow tried the casual approach, "when I took those flies down to the pond. He was there."

"Ian was supposed to be in a mental hospital!" screeched Hannah.

"You are too mad." Meadow's chin began to tremble.

"No I'm not, I'm really not, Meadow. Go on, tell me, I'll be calm. What was he doing down there?"

"Lying on his side. When he talked to me, it gave me a funny feeling. He wanted to play school, but I wouldn't. Then he gave me the knife and said to forget the frogs and practice on him!"

"Good God, little child, what did you do?"

"I *pretended* to do it on him. 'Harder! Harder!' he said, then he took the knife and said, *like this*! And, Ma, he cut himself." She made a line with her finger from the top of her shoulder to the armpit. "He also called me a dumbbell."

"And that's when he threw the knife at you?"

"First I made him madder."

"Oh, Meadow, I'm so sorry! Go on."

"I kept not doing what he told me, so he said I deserved what he was gonna give me. I didn't think he would beat me up because — remember? — you said he wasn't the kind, but I was scared, so I ran anyway. Then something knocked me on the back, and he was still running after me, so that's when I threw the knife in the pond."

Hannah opened her mouth to say what a smart move it was, but the words wouldn't come out. While she'd been in conversation with a spider, Ian had assaulted her daughter. All year long she'd watched over that child, fed her, clothed her, protected her — obviously not — and when it really mattered, she was home talking to herself.

"Don't worry. When he threw it, the knife was all closed up."

In the courage that came from Meadow's presence, she asked the next question, "What happened when he caught you?"

Meadow shrugged as though that part was incidental. "He just let me go. First, he shook me up and down, then he just sorta stopped and put me back down on my feet. He got blood on me! You didn't even see it when I got home!"

"I seem to miss a lot."

"Yeah. I sure am glad. Luckily it wasn't my school clothes. Hey, you wanna hear the song I made up last night? It's about stones and buffaloes."

Hannah felt strong enough to start the car, partly because she was feeling the cold. If Meadow could change the subject at this point, so could she. Stones and buffaloes, stones and buffaloes, she thought, trying to re-channel her mind. You just never know what to expect, do you? Life is beyond all knowing.

"Sing away," she said. "We can't spend the rest of our life talking about 'gone'. Has your microphone disappeared?" Her hands still shook, but she closed them tight on the steering wheel.

"It's right here," said Meadow, taking a deep breath while she flipped the cord out of her way. Then her voice turned soft as a lullaby.

> Stones don't run
> on very fast feet
> like buffaloes run on.
>
> And stones don't fly
> on very fast wings
> like eagles fly on.

"You like it so far?"

"Uh huh."

"I'm not done yet. Here comes the pretty part."

> But stones do sleep
> in very fast ponds
> and don't ever roll on the frogs
> in their sleep
> and don't ever roll on the frogs.

Hannah swallowed. Then instead of crying, she drummed on the steering wheel. "Well, I think it's time someone finally wrote a song about fast ponds, I really do."

"I knew you'd like it. It makes me think of good Indians. That's what it was gonna be about, but I went to sleep before I got there."

Life was plentiful, teeming with order and disorder. Her portion of each seemed roughly equal at the moment.

"What does it make you think of, Ma?"

"Always the same stupendous thing," said Hannah. Swift as an arrow, her mind shot itself across an open plain. She didn't say of Whom it made her think; instead she dared to raise her heart like a lance, and gallop into the midst of battle with a war cry named love. *Every day is a good day to die, Eeeiii!!*

"Buffaloes?" suggested Meadow.

"Sure," said her mother. "It makes me think of every living creature there is, especially buffaloes."

The End

Book II
Counting Down: A Memoir
Rosalie Wolfe

"If I die at night, it will be slapstick all the way." Those were the opening words of an autobiographical novel I wrote some thirty years ago. It is titled *Hannah Wolfe's Blacktime Song*, and I am Hannah. Or rather, I am Rosalie Wolfe, having disguised myself to a certain degree. In the novella I have a daughter named Meadow who is six years old in 1973, as was my real daughter Meadow. I could not bear to disguise a child with so much grace.

This very long short story, or long novella, or short novel seems to me now like a kind of score. Unfortunately, I am unable to speak as a musician; nevertheless, emotionally I feel that I captured my perceptions by scoring them in a kind of way, and now I have pages that seem almost like sheet music, the words to sing, the notes to play. They are there to support my deeper memories, which would today be unavailable to me had I not captured them somehow.

So much that is real, especially the inner movement of life, fades quickly from consciousness. Perhaps it's meant to; but that doesn't make it less real. I called my story fiction to give myself a little room for error. I had to work around the edges of the truth to recreate its center.

Fully realized without benefit of pseudonym, Meadow has flourished as herself. She's been my door into the center of everything; a gift I didn't deserve, but one I needed. I hope this brief memoir will help to fill things in and make the novel more whole. I might add, it was less fun writing than the novel

If *Hannah Wolfe's Blacktime Song* is the ebb, then *Counting Down: A Memoir* is the flow. The first work is uncanny; the second is more mundane, and not so full of anger and sarcasm. I don't mean to imply my present circumstances are mundane; I'm only speaking of this memoir. For me, life in its entirety is still haunting, whether fiction or non-fiction. And slapstick continues to be as good a word for wrestling with God as I know.

In 1948 on a cold Sunday morning in April, I made my appearance in Cincinnati, Ohio, a place I like, but have never loved, so I have no excuse for spending so many years there. I'm pretty sure it says something about my character. If I'm in an uncharitable mood, I'd say it shows how lazy, unimaginative, and insecure I am. But sometimes I think it shows how throughout my life I have been able to take what was given, understanding that every place on Earth is full of hidden riches. I never thought of Cincinnati as home exactly, only as my mother Lucille's home.

At my birth, she had reached the age of thirty-two; she was a fifth grade school teacher who had been told she probably couldn't have children because she didn't ovulate normally. My father was a very handsome dentist of mixed race who (in 1953) dropped dead of a heart attack as I was opening the screen door to leave for school. One minute he was saying he had the worst heartburn of his life, and then he suddenly had neither.

He was only forty-three when he died, a man in the best of health, or so we thought. But now that I think about it, my most common memory of my dad is of him asleep in his overstuffed chair in the evening. Work apparently exhausted him more than seems normal to me now. He'd come home, be silly with me for a few minutes and make me laugh, then fall asleep with his mouth open reading the newspaper.

We said it for years after his death – Jack was a man in the best of health when he died! I've since learned that the men on his side of the family only lived till their forties because of heart disease, and the women only lived till their fifties for the same reason! Here I am, fifty-five-years old, but not much of a meat-eater. If we are only our genes, half of me may try to prove it soon, so I am making a start at non-fiction while I'm still here.

Even my mother, Lucille (Richards) Wolfe, never made it to sixty, dying at age fifty-nine from lung cancer. I'm revealing the biggest secret of her life. No one ever knew, except us her family, that from the moment she got home from work until she went to bed at night, she had a cigarette in her hand. She was totally ashamed of her addiction, thought it was the worst thing a school teacher could do, and made outlandish efforts to hide the habit.

I was ashamed of it as a young child only because she obviously was. Once she told me she'd promised my dad to quit if and when they conceived a child, but she never did – quit, that is. She thought that was why I was born so small, less than six pounds. She confessed this to me when I was ten-years-old. We both cried, then she dried my eyes and lit a cigarette. After that she felt better, but I felt worse, and it wasn't until she noticed my mood that she put it out and was kind enough to feel bad again with me.

Part of me is still angry and disgusted, but those are hard emotions, not worthy of my deeper love. The rest of me is still unbelievably sad. Think of all the discipline she used in not smoking from the time she woke up, not even with her morning coffee, until she came home for the day! I don't think that could be typical of smokers in general. She was like two different women.

What can I say about the second woman? First, that she was the best grade school teacher I ever had. That's right, I insisted on being in her class in fifth grade, and I was so incredibly stubborn about it that all adults concerned concluded there would be no slippery slope if they made an exception to the rule for me, seeing my heart was completely set on it. My emotional need seemed to all of them greater than the danger of elementary school disorganization. I've tried to remember, raising Meadow, that there's an exception to every rule.

Another facet of Lucille's character was how she came alive and was at her best in the classroom. Students adored her and quite willingly accepted being designated "worker bees" who were born to make a fabulous effort. A group task counted for something in her little hive of classroom workers. No one, even when mad or upset, wanted to disrupt the rhythms she put into motion.

Until fifth grade, I had no experience of being called royal. When our turn came, nothing much was asked of us except the usual individual effort, but we did get to put ourselves first as a special privilege, while continuing to consider the greater good. For instance, when it was your turn to be the Royal King or Queen, you got to make decisions about various things. Should we look up a word in the dictionary so everyone would understand it? The Royal Bee could say no, and class proceeded as usual.

But after awhile, you didn't really care so much about the fact that you had real power. It began to feel more important to do the right thing for others. Being Royal, you didn't have to explain your decisions or make excuses; what you decided was your royal privilege. Lucille honored no as well as yes. But she helped you love yes the best. Thinking only of yourself was actually just not that much fun in her class.

The end of the school day was always the high point though, when we had done such a good job that our work was behind us. The Royal Bee would sit in front of the class beside our teacher, Mrs. Wolfe, and we would be read to for a good forty-five minutes. If the Royal Bee decided to read to the class, that was fine. I still remember the voice of a boy reading from *Tom Sawyer*. I actually got a crush on him for one day because of how well he mimicked Tom, and I was inspired to practice my own reading more thereafter.

No one looked down on the less gifted readers, of whom I was one; if students wanted to, they merely designated by Royal Decree that Mrs. Wolfe should serve the hive as reader that day. It felt festive the way we came together to listen to good words. Although my mother and I had just gotten television that year, the listening to Story with a capital "S" was in no way diminished as a pleasure. The two different activities seemed to have nothing in common at all.

Lucille had the best voice. It was full of different nuances and tones, not pure at all. I remember it made me think of turkey gravy with its various flavors so intermingled. Had I known I would later write a memoir, I could have thought of her voice as honey, thereby extending the metaphor of her classroom. But turkey gravy is the truth. That voice made her loved, even for itself alone, blessed as it was by her secret nicotine. It didn't dawn on me until I was grown, (and had listened to other nicotine voices) that hers was probably more compromised than blessed.

Years later, when I got back from my shack in the scenic (gut-wrenching) knobs of Kentucky, Mother and I were both determined to close the gap between us brought on by my prolonged adolescence. Sixteen, seventeen, eighteen, nineteen, when Meadow was born, these were not good years for us except for Meadow herself. I heedlessly went my own way and spouted more opinions than at any point before or after.

Meadow's birth shook me out of my psychic oblivion, and left me on the verge of adulthood for the first time. Giving birth to her made me pay extreme attention to Him. My spiritual senses were sharpened. I became a woman who at least wanted to stop testing the limits in an adolescent fashion. It became important to me to grasp what limits really matter, and why? I felt I needed to *live* the important limits in a testing sort of way. It wasn't about breaking away from something; it was finally about *becoming* something, now I might say *reclaiming* something. That something haunted me. I had to get into it to get past it. There was knowledge in Cincinnati I wasn't able to get, *higher education* in the truest sense of the word.

I had given myself free rein, deeply conscious of my power to do so. But oddly enough, all that brought me was Meadow, a definite yes from the Universe. *Now I didn't feel that was right!* What was God saying to me? Don't grow up? Don't be good? Here, take a huge reward for doing things backwards, and name her after something beautiful I've made, like a meadow or a river or a bird? How dare He? Who did He think I was? And why was He so careless who He handed babies out to? I probably knew how to use the word "whom", but I was too offended at His ways to do it.

I could see that she wasn't really mine except to raise. She belonged to Him. And I had to raise her to His standards? Listen, God, I can't love her enough, protect her enough. Where's my punishment in all this? Haven't you skipped a step? I haven't even found You yet! Of course, right after she was born, I couldn't say that because He showed up.

It was the 1960s, a time of outraged decency in my generation. We wanted things to be fair, to be better than fair. Where have all the flowers gone, and all that? Forget the government, I wanted God to change. I'd given up on the government, which was even more careless of life than God.

When I was little, I used to tell Lucille, "Just spank me, don't talk to me!" That's the trouble I had with God. He was too mild. I had to do something radical like run away from home for awhile. It took about six years to get my nerve up during which time I did nothing interesting or noteworthy, believe me.

I planned to pick this fight with Him and look Him straight in the Eye. I knew I would probably blink first, but I also knew that by physically leaving the city I'd always lived in, something irritable in me would finally settle down and accept Love. He told me it would, and then fogged me up a bit, so the adventure would feel more completely like my own idea.

Anyway, twelve months later when Meadow and I pulled our Dodge Dart into Lucille's driveway, she offered us the two-room apartment above the detached garage where she parked her new Pontiac. Neither of us had seen the other one's car before, and that alone made me a bit shy for a few days. After we started talking, everything was perfect except my cat Antlers preferred to live with Lucille in her very nice and spacious house. He hurt my feelings, but after all, it was his house too, and being a cat, he didn't get a vote about heading south to Kentucky.

Within hours, I'd lucked into the same heavy paper route I'd had off and on for years. That fed us and kept gas in the car. My immediate needs were few, and I even saved money. Heavens! I had all the conveniences except a phone, even had free newspapers seven days a week. I got to catch up with the news. Nixon resigned? J. Norris Simpson never told me that! Nobody did! Finally, I realized how out of it I must have been.

Meadow started second grade, and I had fantasies of Lucille being her teacher in a few years. This did not materialize because it was that year, after we got back, that my mother's health began to fail. It wasn't much that first year. She was a little short of breath, a little sallow. Her cough was chronic. But the second year, when we were still cozy above the garage, Lucille lost a lot of weight, seemingly overnight.

We moved back into her house when she started fainting, and stayed throughout the diagnosis of lung cancer and congestive heart failure. And death. Without much training, I more or less functioned as a hospice nurse during which time I felt unlucky and lucky both. I was losing her daily. Still, because of the fact that I lived on her property so thriftily that I could make do with delivering papers, I was there. How does a daughter manage when her mother is dying in some other state and she has full-time work she can't bend to her own purposes?

It was painful watching Lucille suffer death, but at least I felt sane. Meadow and I were with her, and she was simply at the other end of her own birth process into mortality. To be born is to die, she said, and she did not feel cheated of time. I had to keep watch on my emotions in one area: Smoking caused this to happen sooner rather than later. Behind that thought lay demons of resentment eager to claw at her in anger.

My year in Kentucky held me steady. It was only demons after all. I had tested them, and knew them for what they were. When the attacks raged, I washed her feet with special care, and knew I was completely safe. More important, she was safe with *me*.

We talked a lot. She urged me to sell the house and finance a college education for myself. There also would be enough to save for Meadow's education. Lucille's granddaughter was already being identified at school as a gifted student. In second grade, she read better than I did in fifth, and she loved studying her books. We laughed about genes skipping a generation and surmised that Meadow would grow up to be a teacher too, which she did. Only she became a Mormon and teaches at Brigham Young University. I wonder if Lucille had something to do with that?

It disturbed my mother that college didn't appeal to me. She often asked me why, and in formulating answers to her, I came to understand it better. My sense of life happening around me was very strong already. Every day was a new sort of reading to absorb. Life itself was the only professor I truly appreciated, so why waste money on me? In the old days, not every smart person felt the need to learn more than the basics of reading, writing, and arithmetic. Of course, I wasn't thinking about the computer age at that point, or of any age, not even the old one headed my way.

Some people, not I, know what they want to do when they grow up. They have the world of schools out there waiting to teach them how. How. That very word wants to teach me something right now, but because I'm more like everyone else these days, I hurry past it. Still, I don't forget that behind those three letters, which are just squiggles, there lies a realm of great potentiality and movement which are particular to the mind and body I was fated to use as my instruments of perception. "How" is like a smoke signal; it's full of cogency. Within it lies something pertinent to my own life, if I'm the one who reads it. If I really paid attention to any word, like **how**, for instance, my heart and mind would shift, and I could better move toward my destiny as a human being. There's real life in words. True openings. God didn't call Himself **AM** for nothing.

Lucille sighed in a long and drawn out way when I said things like that.

"My dearest bright-eyed daughter, I'd like to tell you you're taking the path of least resistance in foregoing college, but some*how* I can't. When your life – as it IS – really seems to matter, why not just live it and see what happens, at least for a time?"

What a good mother! But, after all this time, I've had to settle, like everyone else in the world; that's why I hurry past the teaching inherent in even one word, to the relief of my daughter.

All this continued to be strenuous for my dying mother to grasp, and it speaks well of her that she believed me when I reassured her I didn't use LSD in the 1960s. That is true. A certain kind of leisure has always been my mind-altering choice. That, and coffee every morning. If I had my life to live over, I think I would find a way to get myself psychoanalyzed, and then become a psychoanalyst myself. But I doubt I have the generosity of spirit to wade deeply into other minds besides my own.

I think the grief and pessimism I would almost certainly feel for many of my patients would overwhelm me. Reading Carl Jung has always been helpful in getting my bearings. In my thirties I came across something he said to the effect that he could help the sickest psychiatric patient to get better, as long as that person was willing to tell the truth. I took that to heart. A psychoanalyst like Jung unraveled tremendous suffering one lie at a time. But he must have had an extraordinarily optimistic endowment to do it.

Now Meadow, she was born to rally the troops as a professional. She has a Ph.D. in American Literature, and is a specialist in Mark Twain studies. Being a born educator, she had to live a different life than I have. She seems to do it all, and is remarkably good humored. Not only does she teach, but she has two boys and a husband. And she participates fully in her Church.

She objects when I say she does it all, sighing just like Lucille, who, I must say, never deigned to call me corny. What I mean to say in praise of her is that she carries enormous responsibility, and has none of the disturbed and disapproving attitude toward God that I had when He gave me her, one darling child that bowled me over with wonder and worry.

The thing that Meadow has in great abundance is confidence. I think it is her sense of humor, along with that ingrained confidence, that allows her to stay constant in overlooking the imperfection of others. To me, that *is* perfection of a sort. If I could have kept her inside me with all her qualities, I would have made a great psychoanalyst. But God is always pulling us out of each other like taffy, and nobody gets it all. Thus are we born into community.

I have to stop here and ask myself what my reader wants to know next. So far I've said nothing about the years between Lucille's death and Meadow's professorship. I didn't tell you that Antlers died peacefully of great old age, or that I have a second old cat named Dulcinea, who is a gray Persian lump of soft, purring fur. Not to mention the dogs. Animals have been extremely important to me, both in flesh and spirit.

Maybe what I'm putting off writing about is the man who impregnated me soon after high school graduation, Meadow's father. In *Hannah Wolfe's Blacktime Song*, I said that he took the elevator and I took the stairs. I made that up; it sounded like country music. What we are really talking about is, if not a one-night stand, a weekend romance. So I really went and messed things up as only an amateur grownup could. I wish I'd had more common sense than all that sense of the moment.

What happened is this: Lucille had convinced me to enroll in the Cincinnati Art Academy so I could learn weaving or paper making or *something*. I had just begun living not far from our house, which is also in the same Adams Hill neighborhood the school is. I had a roommate named Tansy Clark. She is now a well-known fabric artist exhibiting in Manhattan and other posh places. But then we were both just students, and hardly knew each other.

Lucille had managed to convince me that I needed, at least, to learn about materials. She wasn't referring to fabric, but to stuff, the fabric of things in nature. I had shown no talent as an artist, but I had an attachment to primitive objects and things that I could actually touch with my hands, like animals. So she convinced me that it would be good to get out of my head and into something undeniably real, even as I protested that nothing lasted very long, especially the reality of which she spoke.

My mother saw brilliantly that my hope lay less in distant goals or favorite books, and more in learning to construct something, anything, from the ground up. She really didn't see how productive I was becoming in an interior way (or realize I would later write a novel as she lay dying), but she was definitely launching me in the right direction. I needed to see things with my eyes more, and touch things with my hands, and (ahem) I did!

One Friday night, Tansy and I found ourselves, though underage, at the Blind Lemon where she washed dishes. I don't know if it's still a great bar, but it was then. I was pushing nineteen, a person close to inexperienced in the ways of sex, and no sort of party girl either. I had never so much as tasted whiskey. That weekend was my introduction to rum and Coke.

Because Tansy had me there as her new friend and unofficial helper, we mostly stayed in the back out of sight. No one minded, everything was easy. When she thought she needed a little break, she'd dry her hands and go out on the floor and dance for ten minutes. I followed her example. Pretty soon I found reason to stay on the dance floor because I'd met a young man who danced very, very well indeed. Once he started with me as his partner, he never suggested we switch.

He was old enough to drink, but didn't overdo it. As I watched the crowd get more and more inebriated, I saw him going in the opposite direction. Perhaps that's what seduced me the most. He seemed to get more and more focused and concentrated as a being. I was pretty high and had trouble gauging what another sip of his drink would do. I didn't feel drunk, but I worried that I was.

Would a drunk person notice all the lovely things I was observing in Peter, I wondered? He seemed like the first man, like Adam. No, no, he seemed like a coyote in human form, First Coyote. He had none of my deceased father's jocularity, and under the influence of alcohol, I realized what a serious person I, myself, really was at heart. At one and the same time, he was both gentle and hard; his mouth was full of perfect white teeth, animal teeth. But his eyes were like a supernatural being. I thought he looked at me with tenderness and wisdom.

Well, you say, you were most certainly drunk. All right. Needing fresh air, we left the Blind Lemon to walk in the streets, and we talked about things I can no longer remember, except what comes to mind now. He was in town for his uncle's funeral that had taken place earlier in the day. I remember he said he had flown out with his father, but he would hardly say anything more about it until the next day.

The talking we did was lovers' talk, and at the moment when my physical and mental attraction felt too strong to bear, I said I needed to lie down. I'm pretty sure it was just because my knees were like jelly, but his answer to that was to ask me if I'd like to spend the night with him in a motel room. I gulped and said yes. So it wasn't a hotel, as I said in my novel, just a measly motel. But to me it was like the *First* measly motel, and I remember laughing about the things I was saying straight from my unconscious to both his and God's ear.

I was watching myself. All the lights seemed green, green, emerald green. At the moment I was not held back by even one red or yellow flashing thought. Of course, when morning broke I had a serious, though not horrible, headache. But it didn't do much to lower the threshold of my happiness. He was still just as good to be with minus alcohol. How he felt, I don't know, but he was very sweet to me, and invited me to breakfast at a cafe next door. From there I used the payphone and called Tansy to say I was fine. She reminded me I'd called the night before to reassure her.

I was worried that my mother might drop by our apartment, and I gave Tansy reason to think she would be glad later if she threw Lucille off my scent. Lucille didn't come by or even call, so who knows where she was herself? Often she'd walk the dogs in my direction, but not that morning.

Peter, his last name was Bonavich, sat across from me in a booth in very clear light. We looked at each other with only a hint of shyness and took up talking where we'd left off. He had a dignified face, lean and smooth, with red hair that was basically auburn like mine. But I couldn't at all place his ethnic heritage. I'm some kind of Melungeon mix, a Portuguese, Indian, African, Scots-converso-Jew from the 1600s. I tried to fit him into that rather unknown, but common, category, but it didn't work. "Something is different about you," I said, "but I don't know what." His eyes were dark; almost the color of his hair. A man with auburn eyes? My eyes were blue. I'd given myself brown eyes in the novel just for the heck of it. "Are you Irish? You don't look Irish." He had me on the edge of my seat.

He seemed very reluctant to talk about himself. Finally he made the decision to tell me what it was he thought I was picking up on. "I am one of those mixed breeds," he said calmly. "Even more than most of us."

"Right," I said, thinking of all I was, but eager to hear more. "Are you a Hungarian redskin? Just kidding!"

"My great-grandfather, my mother's grandfather, was Navajo, some kind of minor chief named Lost Five Brothers. My mother tells me that her grandfather's heritage in me is still obvious to her and that it could play itself out for some generations to come. She's not as close to those roots as she would like, so she doesn't say a lot about them; neither do I. But you flew under the radar, and figured it out, didn't you? When you called me First Coyote, I said, damn, she's good."

"Peter, sometimes I know things I don't know I know, that's all."

"Like I'm part Hungarian as well?"

Here is the story as best as I can remember it about Peter Bonavich. He was a soldier stationed in Colorado Springs, Colorado, and his father was a Department of Defense person at NORAD in that underground bunker like a city where serious war was within minutes of being declared at any time of the day or night. My mind reeled from all this. It was not the way I wanted to think of Peter or his parents. His mother was a housewife with children still in school, and she coached tennis part-time, for even younger children, I think. She had the knack of identifying young talent; I think that was it.

I did not know that we had made a baby, so I didn't ask the questions I should have. My questions foolishly didn't even reflect that possibility. I must have thought that since Lucille didn't ovulate normally, I wouldn't either. What I mainly wanted to know is if we would see each other again, and it didn't look good given he had a plane to catch that afternoon. And unlike last night, Peter in the morning was a person obviously upset, as well he should be, by the fact his uncle didn't live through the collision of a tractor trailer slamming the rear end of his car.

It seemed like everything moved fast and broke apart – just what I tried to tell Lucille when she wanted me to get more experience of the undeniably real. One night Peter was there, and the next he wasn't, although he called on Sunday from Colorado to say goodbye. He gave me a phone number, but I knew the meaning of the word goodbye. Dialing that number did not seem like a rational act. I might just as well ask Tansy to break a vase over my head for all the good that telephone number on a scrap of paper was going to be. So on Sunday evening when my mother did show up after supper with the dogs, I went walking with her and acted like everything was just as it should be, intact and good. Which it eventually proved to be.

If you don't mind, or even if you do, I intend to leave all that alone as far as this memoir goes. Nothing is secret, and I would tell anyone about it one-on-one. But if there has ever been a truly sacred part of my life, that was it – from the time I realized that a child was on the way, until she was in my arms. It's as if the world shivered hard and I found myself in another dimension, a place that seemed less opaque than ordinary life. It was a hard, cool shiver that woke me up, then came a wave of something I can't describe, except it felt like God. Even Lucille said she felt overcome when she took Meadow into her arms. (I actually knew I was pregnant less than a month after the motel. I've only been pregnant once, but apparently that's one of my under-utilized gifts, to feel pregnancy early)!

Just because God blesses you, and you feel it and know it, that doesn't mean you have necessarily participated fully. Some part of me was a bystander critiquing Him. Yes, I'd said yes to sex from my heart. But I felt He had a lot of explaining to do, and He wasn't really doing it. I got more and more shrill and discontent inside. Something was taunting me to test Him. When I got my nerve up, I told myself I had nothing to lose but two part-time jobs, my paper route, and a lesser job delivering organic produce to co-op subscribers each month. As for the Art Academy, I had quit. I needed to tell a doctor I was pregnant, so I paid one just after Thanksgiving. That done, things felt official. It was that same season when Meadow and I left for Kentucky some five years later.

Let me return to Lucille's time of dying as a way of getting to other events as well. Meadow was in third grade, and we were permanently in the main house. It had been easy to rent out the garage to an art student. There were six of us: Lucille, Rosalie, Meadow, Antlers, Perkins, and Waggy. Meadow named the one you'd guess she did. Perkins was one of the two earlier dogs we had at the time I started art school. The other dog, George, jumped out the car window one day in traffic and was quickly run over. So when I left for Kentucky, my Mother took Perkins, and I took Antlers, a large yellow tomcat I'd found as a kitten sitting on the curb in front of our house. I liked to tell him I'd found him in the gutter, but I really didn't. When the three of us got back to Cincinnati, we went to the pound for Waggy. It was to help Meadow feel like she had enough of what she wanted. Responsibility? Maybe. She was always a good helper.

While she was sick, Lucille told me, when I asked the question Sebastian asked me, that she had suggested the name of Antlers to me because on her honeymoon, she and my father Jack had stayed at the Antlers Hotel in Colorado Springs. It was just a good luck name for an almost out-of-luck kitten. I always liked it for its non-urban sound. While in Kentucky, I even asked Meadow to draw our cat with antlers. Now, whenever I think of Peter, I can imagine myself honeymooning with him there in Colorado Springs, neither of us saying goodbye. But that thought passes. It remains strange that two different cities connect us.

I digress. The main thing we got done during Lucille's very debilitated year was to discuss her life in depth. I'm only going to call myself stupid once in this memoir, although the reader might feel I could have used the adjective to good advantage at least twice. I stupidly did not write down anything she told me. I thought I had an excellent memory. When you're still in your prime, you just do not appreciate the fact that brains age. The face, yes, that's a worry, but the brain is supposed to take care of itself. So even though I remembered her stories for a long time, they did not stay with me the way I expected. But here goes.

She was born Lucille Richards in Hubbard, Ohio, just over the border from Pennsylvania. Her various family members had scattered throughout the counties on the other side of Ohio, little by little, ever since her great-grandparents, named William and Ester Bayles (of English Yorkshire heritage), had made it to Illinois. In 1846–47, the Bayles family was leaving Illinois, crossing the Mississippi at Nauvoo in the winter. They were part of the Mormon emigration fleeing persecution. It drove many such families West before they could adequately prepare.

William and Ester left with a large body of the Saints, but didn't have the wherewithal to keep going. They just managed to escape the reach of their enemies before William died. Ester buried him someplace near Montrose, Iowa, then struggled to live as best she could in that area the rest of her life. Her descendants did well enough for themselves, and some of them continued to identify as Mormons. All those ancestors who never made it to Utah seem somewhat less well-defined and scattered to me, but I'm seriously delving into it.

Lucille's mother, my Grandmother Richards, died before I was born. It was the Spanish Flu epidemic of 1918 that took her; and her husband died in Montrose, Iowa when I was five. Lucille drove back for his funeral without me, bringing home a flower from his casket as a token gift. She'd pressed it in a book so it wouldn't look dead, just dry.

My mother's dad was the last of a lot of old relatives Lucille grew up around. She had an aunt and uncle in Carthage, Illinois who according to family lore were the grandchildren of rabid Mormon haters. I don't know. But the facts are that when this aunt and uncle got up in years, they crossed the Mississippi and moved in with Lucille's father. Four people shared the house, and Lucille was the one who ran it, because her dad was by then a heavy drinker and not in the best of health.

She grew up doing the best she could for everyone, and even managed to attend a teacher's college. I got the picture of three old relatives depending on one young woman, my mother. I imagine a dying hive of bees. As she put it, everything had to be said twice, and the second time, r.e.a.l s.l.o.w. I can just imagine her starting to smoke so late in the evening they never even guessed.

And then, and then, and then: She did what lots of young people do, leave. But her leaving guaranteed a professional job and paycheck, unlike my departure (and that of our ancestors – hounded out of Illinois). In Cincinnati, no doubt, she blossomed in many ways. I sincerely hope she had some fun for a change. She did not practice any form of Mormonism, but I realize now what I didn't then. In many ways she remained very Mormon in her propensity for humble community service.

Before too long, she met a striking, Episcopalian dentist whom she married. She had integrity, and the desire to give of herself and work hard. It so happened that my father (whose skin was often described as "rather dark") had a life that pulled her into some social standing in the community. He was not part of the war effort, but instead took on a larger practice than he wanted as other dentists in town joined the Army Dental Corp. My parents were, as far as I know, very happy, even though World War II meant serious sacrifice for many people. I was born to the manor, in a circuitous way.

She told me about her honeymoon, that they went to Colorado and Arizona and took mules down the Grand Canyon. Deciding that the air was too thin for them, they returned to Cincinnati and decided to play bridge and golf instead of travel. They'd seen enough, and thought that high-quality coffee table books would do it from there on out. Please excuse my snobbishness, which is evident even to me, and unmerited.

Because of them, I have always turned to the public library for practical knowledge. That's where I found books on nursing and other subjects I thought might interest my mother as she "rested" in bed. Because she was so ill, I think, I only had one success. That was with *The Adventures of Huckleberry Finn.* She had read it, of course, but not that many times. She said the school would never let her introduce it! And Meadow and I had never read it. The three of us had as much fun as it's possible to have in such a situation.

Meadow was a sly mimic and portrayed each character as I read. I really had to stop her in the middle of her antics because Lucille couldn't breathe well enough when she began to laugh. It became a cough and then worse. So Meadow learned a lot about comic timing, which she swears she couldn't teach without.

Then, when they were both down for the night, I began writing *Hannah Wolfe's Blacktime Song*. It was not easy going. The life I lived in Kentucky barely stayed in the past. Sometimes I'd be lost in writing and Lucille would cough, and for some moments I'd feel like my Kentucky landlord and I were sharing a house. Even though the writing helped me escape from pain, it hurt too.

Lucille made it through Christmas and almost to spring, but she died before the earth warmed up. February 28, 1975 was an average day, but also a day of Creation different from all others, just as she was herself. She had been in hospice care for the last month, which I hoped to avoid, but she was determined that it would be better for all concerned, as she put it, if neither Meadow nor I witnessed her demise. Seeing my father die qualified me in her mind for an exemption.

Her church, The Episcopal Society of Christ Church, saw to the service, and the pews seemed amazingly full to me. All along people had dropped by to help out here and there, but I wasn't prepared for so many mourners waiting in the wings. Of course! She had mentored many students over the years. Also, she had apparently spoken with many friends when I wasn't around, because it was clear others knew what she wanted in terms of music and interment.

I never pretended she wasn't dying; I faced right up to it. But there were certain conversations I had a hard time negotiating, and she shielded me more than I realized. Meadow got it right. She cried from her head to her toes at the service, then right before the recessional, she blew her nose loudly and stood to read a poem she'd written the day before. She told me it was actually a song, but she was too old and sad to act like her invisible microphone was real. Nor did she wish to sing with an actual one.

Here is her poem. She only asked for help with some of the spelling; the words are all hers.

There was a time
When it was fine
To give myself to singing
And Lucy sang, and sang, and sang
Until my head was swimming.
Now her voice has gone away
And left my song collapsing
And left my song collapsing.

By Meadow Wolfe, age 8 (almost);
Lucille's best granddaughter

After the poem and the stately recessional, singing! And no dry eyes. It's new to me that Lucy sang so much, but Meadow said it happened when I was delivering the newspapers.

I'm trying to remember other books we read, but I can only remember one. It was *A Marvelous Work and a Wonder* by LeGrand Richards. I picked it up at a yard sale because I loved the title, and he had my mother's maiden name, Richards. It was over all our heads. Not too many things nonplus me, but that one did. I liked his be-of-good-cheer tone though. Sometimes when I was writing my story, and I felt pretty miserable, I'd reach for LeGrand Richard's book, and I'd get a strong sense that my own feeble effort as a seeker was also a marvelous work and a wonder, even if no one ever knew what I was about. The title itself always comforted me, and to tell the truth, I wrapped our copy of that book in velvet, and laid it in Lucy's coffin with a little goodbye note. Maybe I knew something I didn't know I knew.

This is not to say we neglected to read the Gospels, especially over Christmas. But we read shyly, and there wasn't any discussion. Each of us listened in our own way and at our own heart's pace. It was just right. Meadow, of course, did comment occasionally. Then her grandmother and I both explained things about Jesus. Perhaps because of the season, we talked in a manger sort of hush. We also held back our presents that year, delighting in small items we had found or remembered we had. Our feelings were extremely tender and in need of the gentlest release. Death was in the house, and we tiptoed around him, but he was more like an uninvited friend than a foe.

So perhaps I've filled things in. When spring came, the world had to be renegotiated. I actually stopped Meadow going out to play one day because she went out too quietly, as if Lucy were sleeping. I said, "Meadow, get back in here and slam that screen door like a good girl!" Her mouth fell open. "Right now, little girl! Give it a big thwack!" She just looked at me until she got it, and wow did she slam it hard. It was our first happy moment since the death. I looked up at the ceiling. "How's that?" I said aloud to Lucille. I, too, felt like a good girl.

I went from having no financial security, to having quite a lot, because there was a sizable insurance policy. It didn't seem to me like the house needed to be sold. It was completely paid for, and I had money in the bank. So we just settled in and down. Within a year of Lucille's death, I had a boyfriend, my first since Peter, who hardly deserves that appellation.

This fellow's name was Eul Choi, and it was over Christmas that we really got to know each other. He spent a full two weeks with Meadow and me. He lived in Columbus, not Cincinnati, which made the relationship unusual. He was in graduate school doing two doctorates, one in physics and another in mathematics, so it was sort of like being someone's mistress; he was not married, but neither was he exactly mine. Primarily, he belonged to his studies.

I wasn't sure I wanted him for keeps, but he was in all ways, until the end, a fine addition to my life. He probably needed a humdrum person, someone to unwind with after hours of abstract labor. I never knew exactly what he saw in me. What I saw in him was a high degree of competency and a pleasant disposition.

I met him at an outdoor concert at the park in town. I think he told me he'd gone fishing with some friends, and then there was this girl the friend wanted to look up. You know, just the happenstance of life. His parents were Korean immigrants, but he'd come to this country as such a small child, he couldn't even remember Seoul or his relatives there.

He and I were together off and on for about five years. The first three were the best, then he finished his studies and left for post-doctoral work for a year. He came back to Ohio for another year and we saw each other at intervals, which steadily lengthened. At some point, past when I should have realized it, I woke up and knew that he was leaving me without saying goodbye.

Which would I prefer: Peter's abrupt withdrawal and goodbye, or Eul's lengthy withdrawal leaving it off? You are right. I prefer Peter's. He made me feel less like a fool, and it showed a kind of manliness I respect.

Eul might someday read this, and because I know his love of privacy, I hesitate to tell you more about him. Obviously, he spent huge amounts of time thinking about physics and math. Those are foreign patterns of thought that are largely still dormant in my psyche. And I mean no disrespect when I say he wasn't particularly interesting to talk to. So it's best just to say what was left in his wake; at least two things permanently transformed Meadow's and my lives.

Before I mention those in more detail, let me say that I very much doubt the reverse was true. All I had to give him was a kind of nothing, and when the time came, he left me, according to rumor, for a much more accomplished woman who was a gourmet cook and played the cello professionally. The friend of Eul's (who passed this information on to me) added that Eul wanted all his children to be biologically his own. That hadn't occurred to me because he was always so good to Meadow. His loss, in my opinion.

Eul taught me to meditate Vipassana style, which is very simple and unencumbered. By that I mean, you won't find martial or religious appendages to it. I thought, being so introverted, that I already knew about my inner world. But this style of meditation taught me more. Meadow still practices it, and so do I.

The other good thing was that he remodeled Lucille's house, turning the back kitchen area and upstairs bedrooms into a very wonderful flat for renting out. This improved my financial security. Actually, over the years, Meadow and I went back and forth between the lower and upper living spaces because I found them both so pleasant to inhabit. Looking down from a high place has always pleased me, that's why I liked the apartment above the garage so much. Thank you Eul.

I'm trying to think if there's a third thing, and nothing comes to mind. Eul's absence, once I recovered from feeling like a dope, has been a benevolent state, unlike Peter's, whose exit continues to itch and tingle. For Meadow, Eul always remained a visitor from Columbus, but now I see how inevitable it was that he would become some sort of father figure. I see now that even though she gained, she lost, and the blame lies with me.

She turned fourteen the year he failed to reappear or call. She was already a young woman, having made it through major physical change the year before with little emotional turmoil. At fourteen she stood taller than I did. Even then her nature was confident.

Then it happened. Ready for her first flight out of childhood, she came home one day and announced that she was going to join The Church of Jesus Christ of Latter-day Saints, and I was invited to the Baptism next week, and would I please fix dinner for the missionaries because they were "extraordinarily" interested in meeting me.

As she hurriedly began preparing the groundwork for something exciting she wanted to tell me, I had rapidly started to formulate a curfew policy for someone only fourteen. I had moved from 9:30 pm to 10:30 pm, then back to 10 pm, remembering in seconds my own first date that had been a lot to handle. I had hoped to put her off till sixteen, but already knew that was a lost cause, because her friends were already getting rings from their new steady boyfriends.

"You're already baptized," I said.

"I know it, but this is another one that, in my opinion, may or may not be necessary, but I want it very much, and the Church says it *is* necessary, so even if I didn't want it as such, which I do, I'd have to do it in order to be a Mormon."

"Hmm."

"What does 'hmm' mean?"

"Gimme a minute or two to think."

"Mom! I just want to talk!"

So it was going to be about religion, not boys. I could see how she might come by it naturally given the person I was, and what I'd done, both well and poorly. And, of course, Lucille's heritage might be a factor, not to mention that I myself had read to her about those folks. But I didn't think we were going to meet any live ones.

"Are they free for supper tomorrow?"

"They are always free."

"Okey dokey." I took a long, smooth breath from the Dan Tian, and years of meditation came to my rescue. I also prayed "Please God Help Me."

The next evening I was introduced to two clean, polite young men in black suits and ties with rectangular name tags identifying them as Elder Prosser and Elder Richards. Richards again! It must be a Mormon name for sure. So I turned to Elder Prosser and asked him if he was very far from home. "How far is it to San Bernadino?" he grinned. My middle-aged heart skipped a beat. He was adorable.

Throughout the evening, we pretty much stuck to the subject of the Plan of Salvation and the rite of Baptism. They liked to see whole families join at once, so they hoped there might be a way for me to join with (or shortly after) Meadow, who would need my permission to make it official because of her age.

Did these guys think that anyone, in a hundred years, would just up and join their Church? I answered my own question looking at Meadow. I kept trying to catch her being flirtatious, but that was a dead end. This apparently was about Church, God, and Jesus Christ, a sort of musical trio now that I think of it!

Some of the things that came out of those young men's mouths were their own inspirations and heartfelt sentiments, and other things were scripted. That made them sound like bad actors, but it was fascinating to observe. They'd be themselves, in character, here, here, gone, gone, gone – here, here. I'd forget what we were talking about because of it.

I liked the way Meadow interacted with them. Unlike me, she stayed focused on the subject, and she was both direct and real. It was sort of like she had gone to the store for paint and was really interested in what she could learn about color, texture, drying time, and technique. It made me think of Lucille.

I hope Meadow wants to tell that whole story someday. As for me, I will just say that she did get baptized, I did attend; I got somewhat teary and did feel a tremendous and genuine flow of love and joy in the room. My Vipassana side felt right at home, even as it had in the early, more agitated days of my practice. All sorts of opinions were in motion. My mind was like wet clothes flapping in the wind. But I didn't get triggered. I also kept my "Please God Help Me" prayer front and center, and somehow life seemed right on course in the same strange way as usual. That was in 1981. I didn't join shortly after Meadow, and I still haven't joined, but there is nothing holding me back except a prompt from God: "Go ahead-Jump in." That's not to say I believe it all, even if I decide to join. But I believe in *them*.

I've lived with Mormons in my life for so long that I know there is nothing to fear. The Church is like a big, mostly wonderful, family. There's serious love in the Church, all the way from the top to the bottom. One of the first things that hooked me was that love. There is much more of that than anything else. Even as a non-member, I was part of the mix, and I came to care about all sorts of people who were trying hard to listen to the Gospel in their lives. I define the Gospel somewhat differently, but that's how families are. No one thinks alike. There is formal Mormon teaching, but I've also heard the President of the Church say that he personally thinks that if anyone has had a deep experience of Jesus Christ, the rest of Salvation will work itself out.

That begs the question of what happens if someone doesn't look to Jesus as Lord. How do I know? I'm much more worried about those of us who call ourselves Christian, but who sin a lot and don't even know it. Help me, God, to not sin! Help me to learn love among others for whom it is also the highest Commandment! Save me from the errors in myself by giving me a deeper understanding of Jesus and His Way. As for enemies, teach me how to love them. It's not about squiggles on a page, after all. It's the love and brotherhood that counts, or so I say, not being a Mormon, only being me this far along and no farther.

Meadow and I have had many conversations over the years about why the Church is not quite right for me. It's partly we're mismatched. Mormons are so extroverted and busy in the world, whereas I'm introverted and busy within, extending the mission field inside myself. How can we preach Christ risen to the world when half the time, He isn't even risen in ourselves? It's one thing to get baptized twice, and another to be a transformed being who is slow to anger and quick to forgive.

Meadow says that obviously the inner and the outer go together. She says the Church needs all kinds of people, and she wonders if I fear that I'm the kind of person who will get angry and then be slow to forgive, so I avoid the challenge? What! Me avoid an inner challenge? She may be right. I don't suffer fools gladly, fool that I am. I am just plain uncomfortable as an extravert. I dislike busyness, and see many things as not essential.

"I understand and forgive you," says my daughter. "Now join the Church, and let others understand you or not, but forgive you and love you."

If I'm a perplexing challenge to others, that's a good thing. It requires virtue to deal with me. And if I don't believe that Mormons desire to grow in virtue and compassion as a people, then I should just leave the Church alone entirely. Of course, Meadow knows it's too late. I do believe in their commitment to love of God and love of neighbor. I witness them anxiously engaged in doing good. They are worker bees, and just don't find it that much fun thinking only of themselves.

I wish Mormons didn't eat so much sugar. It's not good for them! And they tend to make all sorts of doodads that they give to each other to show love. What a griper I am! And there's that scripted side to them. But I am not so superficial that I can't see beyond that. As I say, we're somewhat mismatched. Fundamentally, I respect the H-E-Double-Toothpicks out of them. And they have been accommodating, allowing me, with their usual good humor, to remain an "investigator" year after year. The truth is, I was born an investigator, and when I join the Church, I'll still be one.

I've told Meadow that one thing I do not care for in the Saints is their *exclusive* use of the King James version of the Bible. There are so many good modern translations available that I'd accept consulting other works. But it was in use when Joseph Smith organized the Church in 1830, and the Book of Mormon came to him in language much the same as the original King James, so the two works are somewhat necessarily paired. Still in all, I read Scripture to understand what God might be telling me through ancient text that many people died to preserve, translate, and pass on. It is *meaning* I want to explore in all its forms. So the King James is part of that, but so are more modern texts. But here again, I'm just mismatched, because the Latter-day Saints love their Scriptures in a way that reveals to me how truly the old language speaks to them, and helps them feel a burning in the bosom for Our Father. But once it's there, it's there, even reading revised translations, at least for me.

"I'm just different," I tell Meadow over and over again. And I can hear her reply, "I wish you could really understand that we're *all* different! They just don't make such a big deal about it as you do." She's right. Mormons lay the emphasis on what we have in common, and find joy in building that up and enlarging it. And the Church somehow trusts that each conscience is strong enough to hold its own individually.

One of the biggest goals of the brothers and sisters is, as I see it, to help each other and the children develop a strong and authentic personal sense of direction. Leadership at every level is the goal. Followers are helped in every way to learn to lead themselves and others, and those who would abrogate responsibility are seen as passive. I am not passive, I'm active! But to some I appear passive because I'm not a busy extravert.

So you see my dilemma, and perhaps my blind spot as well. I've been so lucky with my daughter, whose personality finds an easy fit, even though she is known as an outspoken woman. But she's all Mormon in the most inclusive and best sense. She doesn't take herself too seriously, or her neighbor either, whether high or low. But she takes the Plan of Salvation seriously, and has found it as true as anything she knows. And she loves, loves, loves her Church.

I've been paying attention for years to her, and to sisters like her, and they are really something. There is so little gossip, so little backbiting; they are about their Father's business, but not in a holier-than-thou way. They struggle to do right, as though they know there just isn't time to do wrong. I get it! I'm just different. I need to go slow; I just don't have time to fool around with hurry of any sort.

Let me change the subject completely. Without going into too many details of my daughter's life, I think I would be allowed to touch on the subject of her father a little more. At a certain point, as a Mormon, Meadow was given the opportunity to prepare the basic pedigree sheet used for Temple work. The Church of Jesus Christ of Latter-day Saints does baptisms for the dead, everyone knows that. Anyway, Mormons fill out a four-generation sheet that shows a person's heritage up to and including all sixteen great-grandparents, who are our closest ancestors. All the dead are an important part of our families. I, myself, believe in a very large Communion of Saints that even the Episcopal Church makes reference to in its liturgy.

I came easily into understanding the role that ancestors play for Mormons. I read someplace many years ago that the American Indians believed in honoring the dead seven generations back, and serving the children seven generations forward. This is a deeply ethical vision, and I accept it with my whole heart. It seems so obvious to me that not being short-sighted is part of being ethical. How can it be otherwise? Just because I forgive my neighbor for something today is not enough. The present is not enough, even though it's all we have. But as I see it, we must pull the past and the future into the present moment where decisions are made. *Then* our lives can be abundant, and we can bless those surrounding us in whatever direction, forward or backward. Certainly my great-great-great-grandmother, a stranger to me, Ester Bayles, blessed me by passing her "attention to God" genes down. And certainly without her and her exact life, full of missteps and bad decisions, as well as good decisions and good deeds, I would not be alive at all. How is that not a tremendous blessing?

So here is Meadow. Obviously, she had a kind of problem. When she joined the Church, she and I only knew her father's name and his approximate age. I doubted that he was even born in Colorado since he and his family were there on military assignments. One-half of Meadow's family tree was essentially blank. And this man did not even know that Meadow existed. He still doesn't. Peter Bonavich, if you are still out there, please get in touch!

What has happened, is that we think we might have found him through genealogy searches, so she has on paper a partially completed, but not verified, paternal ancestry. I would have called to see if he was the right Peter Bonavich, but Meadow has resisted. First, he may not be up to the shock. Besides that, Meadow, herself, is not ready. So Peter may or may not remain gone.

My daughter has become almost wholly a part of her husband's family without ever letting go of me. And they are an admirable, continually expanding, group of Saints. She married in the Salt Lake Temple, February 28, 2000 (Lucille's day and month of death to give it happier overtones). Her husband is a man I couldn't be happier about. His name is James Dent, and he's an art historian. He and Meadow both have excellent jobs in Provo, and two little boys. She teaches American Literature, specializing in Mark Twain (mostly as a private scholar), and James is a curator for the L. Tom

Perry Special Collections at the BYU library. She and “Jay”, as she calls him, have a lot of laughs, and more creative work than they can ever accomplish.

Did I say yet that I left Cincinnati some years ago, and moved to Salt Lake City? It was after the wedding. For years, I just couldn’t let go of the Episcopal Church of my youth. Although I like to say I travel light, I couldn’t seem to do without Episcopalian liturgy and that regular repetition throughout the year of Christ’s life circling from start to finish in readings so ancient and venerable. No one reads to me like the Episcopal Church.

Once I heard a Mormon say that our progression is like an airplane in flight. If it’s not moving forward, it’s falling. An airplane? The Holy Spirit has been experienced as a dove, but never as an airplane (in my experience). I worship like birds fly, not like a plane. But I do believe in going forward, and I sort of know what the speaker meant: Onward Christian Soldier. I’m a pacifist, but I can still sing that hymn and mean it in the inner way. My encounter with the Kingdom of Heaven has been a violent one. Inside myself, I haven’t had much combat leave, but I’ve found the peace of an old warrior, having done my psychic duty. I know a peace that surpasses all understanding.

I like being in Salt Lake rather than Provo because it’s more diverse. Yes, Meadow, I know Provo is diverse too. The upstairs apartment I live in is similar to the one Eul created in Lucy’s house. It looks east toward the Temple, and is within walking distance of downtown. I live in a neighborhood called the “Avenues” that, classy as it sounds, is really shabby to the right degree.

There’s a hostel nearby, and at night I like to sit on my balcony and watch the nightlife below me. My cat Dulcinea keeps me company. She licks her paw, and washes her ear, twice. Then, like a refrain, she does it again.

After so many years of saying no, it feels good to say, well, yes. I'm ready to jump. Tonight, as I finish this up, the presence of Jack and Lucille is in the air I breathe. My baptism is next Saturday, and I expect them to come and find a way to let me know it. As I write these words, Dulcinea looks up and meows at me. She says, "I'm here." Antlers too. Even Meadow's invisible microphone seems to be hovering somewhere close this evening. I reach out for it and pull in a moth. It's getting too dark to see, but that no longer matters. I open my hand and sing.

The End

"Let every creature
rise and bring
peculiar honors to
our King" — old hymn

A Letter to Rosie

Bordeaux, France
December 29, 2003

Dearest Rosie,

I hope this letter gets to you. I haven't heard that any of my letters arrived anywhere. Write me back EXPRESS, forget the cost. This is my second letter to you, BTW. The first one was lengthy; this won't be, alas.

I've settled in well, as we both knew I would. At the Barchillon's home and at Daniel's table, one wants for nothing. All five of them were home. The two boys still live at home, but Michelle now lives in Paris and works at a stressful marketing job. She came back here for the holidays and promptly got a bad cold on arriving. That usually happens to me too when I change environments, but not this time. I know, I know. I'll come home with Michelle's cold and give it to everyone!

I haven't got much done because of the rain, e. g., wanted to visit the home of my current heartthrob, Michel de Montaigne, but Anita and Daniel know so many charming walks to distract one from "projects." And when the rain stops (still chilly though), I want to be outside, not inside making notes or thinking of research.

Yesterday we picnicked on a hillside high above the confluence of the Dordogne and the Garonne rivers north of Bordeaux. We ate outside a house built into a cliff. I thought of you and your love of sweeping views, but it was a serious climb up crumbling old stairs. The Barchillons are in such good physical shape!

I felt so French as we picked bay leaves and rosemary sprigs, and on the way home we stopped to do a little wine "tasting" (as opposed to swallowing). I was an ignoramus about the wine and didn't offer any comment beyond "robust", a word I seemed to remember might work on that occasion. We used handsome cuspidors for spitting. It made Emma Smith come to mind, her asking Joseph for a Revelation about spitting on the floor. So in a sense, both you and Emma were my invisible companions yesterday, which was nice. It is interesting to realize that she was actually no more invisible than you, even though dead!

It's hard for Daniel that I don't drink, when his house wine is so lovingly made. He impishly says I need to be more wicked. I try to be as wicked as I can for his sake; forget that he doesn't notice.

Oh how I wish that my French were better! I'm always cracking jokes about how poor it is, but my ability to make people laugh here is poor as well. Luckily I can still make Henri and Benoit laugh hard by pretending to speak better French than I'm able. I slip into gibberish accents so fervent that they lose it, and then they imitate English by making hard chewing sounds. We must growl a lot as Americans. I love those boys. Living in the USA for awhile has definitely given them the needed comic edge.

Well, I thought this would be short, but I have to tell you my fantasy of a fun assignment for a class of upper level students. I could ask for a paper comparing and contrasting three men. It's a bold idea, like the men themselves, or so I could argue. The first man could be Montaigne (internationally famous), the second, Mark Twain (internationally famous), and the third is LeGrand Richards. Three men, three categories: war, storytelling/lying, and attitude toward religion based on quotations from research. That would make them squirm intellectually. I might get one brilliant paper, who knows? And I would have a blast reading them all. Or I could be a good girl and stay in the box (in which I'm deliriously happy, or delirious, I'm not sure which with so little sleep). You usually enjoy my more creative ideas, so there it is. James would have good feedback on where to point them for efficient research on Richards.

Next subject! James called to say that he and the little guys are doing fine. Between his mother, his aunt, and our roster of babysitters, no one is seriously overworked. Peep had a cold, but no fever. I miss them all; that's the hard part about traveling. But this trip was his idea, darling man of mine. He would have enjoyed Rosa Bonheur's portrait and horses at the musées. She's the woman who painted Buffalo Bill when he toured France.

Quickly now. Anita's mother, Benedicte Dupuy, whom I finally just met, still writes poetry at age 81. Bordeaux has yet to discover this treasure in its midst! Anyway, Anita showed me one of her poems from WWII years that she thinks you'd like especially. She suggests it carries your themes, and I concur. Anita has penciled in a rough translation in English, which she apologizes for, but I know I couldn't do as well.

Also, again through Anita (so appreciative of America), I've discovered Slim Critchlow, a long ago, very cool, cowboy singer. She heard him on late night radio(?) and wrote the station. Call this number to order us both a copy of the CD. I didn't want to accept a pirated version, which she found amusing. Nevertheless, please buy us both the album "Crooked Trail of Holbrook." I promise you'll love it. 1-888-274-6654. Arhoolie Records, El Cerrito, CA. She can't make out a lot of the lyrics, so we've been listening together. It takes an experienced ear to get old-timey cowboy lingo.

Enuf. Gotta get moving along. All this handwriting proves once again how much I love my mother. No email for her! Meadow, your Forever Mouse

P.S. When am I to visit Plum Village? It's in this general area, I know ….

P.P.S. Home soon. Stay well.

Portique, a French poem with English translation, by Bénédicte Dupuy

x / My avid and miserable desire
That all things would (or should) not exist in vain
in the eternal time

Portico

Portique

« Passing through nature to eternity » (Shakespeare)

x. « ....mon désir avide et misérable
Que tout ne soit pas vain dans le temps éternel »
(H. de Régnier)

Through (or by) this summer threatened by snow	Par cet été que guette la neige	
Through this sun	Par ce soleil que guette la nuit	threatened by night
Through this love	Par cet amour qui se désagrège	which crumbles
This memory threatened	Ce souvenir que guette l'oubli	by oblivion
Through this reflection	Par ce reflet sans retour	without returned image
On a birch grove	Sur un bouquet de bouleaux	
Through this sweet	Par ce doux rayon de jour	ray of light
Escaping over waters	Qui s'évade sur les eaux	
Through this frivolus	Par cette caresse frivole	caress
Like a breeze	Dont la brise effleure mon front	brushing against my forehead
Through this butterfly	Par ce papillon qui s'envole	which takes off
Through this refrain	Par ce refrain qui s'interrompt	which stops
Through this moment	Par cette minute de grâce	of grace
Through this instant	Par cet instant qui m'a quitté	already gone
Through all things	Par toutes choses qui passent	that (which) pass
I shall enter	- J'entrerai dans l'éternité	in eternity.

(La Barthe, 5-IX-1945)

An Afterword from the Dead

I was a damn fool and a careless one at that, but let me tell you, I survived it. Hell of a thing, even my work survived. Much of it was the product of the foolery of which I speak. I have to say, though, that it was more than convenient that I chose to write. I know now that I would have found a way to go to the Devil without it.

Susie said I ought to crack a joke so you'd know it was me. I'm dismally fatigued with being sly to get my point across, so I've moved around to indirect. That's in keeping with the precincts I now inhabit.

Take a look at the character of Horace Bixby and his magnificent navigation of a steamer through the Mississippi shoals in the dead of night. Now there's a job so well done that Señor Savior Himself couldn't have done it better. It's a wonder that I know for a fact.

Just keep in mind it's all in the piloting. No drunkards nor writers need apply for that job, but they don't belong in steerage either. No, let them stay up on deck where the action is to tell the Story, as Miss Rosalie calls it. Listen, and you won't go wrong.

Samuel Clemens-Mark Twain, God's humble and obedient servant, taking his leave for the good of all. Hallelujah!

LaVergne, TN USA
19 August 2010
193906LV00003B/2/P